# JILL

## THE SABELA SERIES BOOK 4

## TINA HOGAN GRANT

Edited by Crystal Santoro Editorial Services: https://chrissyseditorialservices.org/

Cover Design by T.E.Black Designs – http://www.teblackdesigns.com

Visit The Author's Website

www.tinahogangrant.com

❀ Created with Vellum

# CHAPTER 1

## JILL

*I* heard footsteps coming towards where I sat at my desk in the reception area of the dental office. I looked up, surprised to see Claire. "What does she want?" I mumbled under my breath. I have nothing to say to her. We've hardly spoken two words in the years we have worked together, which has been over three.

The last time was over five days ago, and it was more of an argument when Travis, my ex, made an unannounced visit and told me he and Claire were dating.

I tried to avoid her by returning my focus to the computer screen in front of me. But we were the only two people in the room, and it was impossible. So I didn't acknowledge her when she approached my desk—silence settled between us as I remained fixated on my screen.

"Jill, we need to talk," Claire said in a sharp tone.

I didn't look up and snapped at her, "I'm busy." What could she possibly have to say to me that I would care about? I wondered. Is she here to rub it in my face that she is now Travis's girlfriend? I questioned myself.

Claire released a heavy sigh. "Jill, this will only take a minute of your time. Will you please look at me?"

Her tone was forceful, and I reluctantly made eye contact with her. As usual, she was dressed in her light blue scrubs, wore no makeup, and her black-framed glasses dominated her face. My first thought was, what does Travis see in her? She's nothing like me. I looked her up and down—still unable to understand why he dumped me for her. Yeah, we hadn't been getting along, and our love-life was non-existent, but damn, we'd been together four years. We had a history, and he had thrown it all in for her. I don't get it. Even though I no longer loved Travis. I don't even know when I stopped loving him; it's still bullshit that he chose Claire over me.

"What do you want?" I asked, matching her tone.

She rested her forearms on the counter and leaned in. "I wasn't planning on telling you this without Travis here, but I refuse to go through another episode of hiding secrets from you. I didn't like it the first time Travis and I started dating, and we were afraid to tell you. So I'm not doing it again. The minute I walked through that door this morning, I felt uncomfortable just like before."

She wasn't making any sense. "Look, I'm busy. What is this about Claire?"

She took a deep breath. "I wanted to tell you from the horse's mouth before you heard it from anyone else." She paused and took in another breath. "Travis proposed to me over the weekend, and I said yes."

My jaw dropped, and my body fell back against my seat. "What! He proposed to you." I shook my head in disbelief. "But you've only been dating for a few months, right?" I asked, still shocked by the news.

Claire nodded. "Almost three."

"And he proposed to you already? I was with him for four god damn years, and not once did he bring up marriage? What the hell?"

Claire creased her brow. "What are you jealous of? I'm only telling you because it's the right thing to do. It wouldn't be right if you heard it from someone else." Claire added.

I shook my head and folded my arms. "No, I'm not jealous. What gives you that idea? Why are you rubbing it in my face that you are going to be Travis's wife? I honestly don't care. But I don't understand why you guys are in such a rush to get married."

Claire rolled her eyes. "I'm not trying to rub it in your face. You're the one that complained about Travis not bringing up marriage with you. I honestly thought this was a good idea to come and tell you before someone else did, but I can see how it was a mistake."

I had enough and raised my voice. "Claire, what do you want me to do? Be all happy for you and give you a big hug like we are best friends. Well, I can't, okay. Last week I found out the two of you are dating, and then five days later, you tell me you are getting married. Travis and I may have had our differences, and yeah, I'll admit, I treated him like shit towards the end, and I wanted out just as much as he did." Tears pooled in my eyes. I fought to keep them from spilling. "But when he left me, even though I knew it was going to happen, it still hurt. I mean, it really hurt. I played like I didn't care, but after our last fight and when he walked out that door, I knew it was over, and it suddenly became so surreal." I wiped a tear that had escaped my eye. "It's just weird, okay. We both work here, and you are a constant reminder of Travis. How am I supposed to move on when I have to be reminded that he dumped me for you every time I see you?"

Claire moved her hands to her hips and shook her head. "What are you talking about, Jill? He didn't dump you for me. You even said a few minutes ago that you knew it was over before he ended it. Even if he hadn't met me, you know damn well you guys had no future. You are just using me as an excuse. Look, I'm sorry seeing me upsets you and reminds you of your breakup, which was bound to happen anyway, but you won't have to worry about it soon."

"Why? Is there something else you need to tell me?" I snarled.

"As a matter of fact, there is. I'll be giving my two weeks' notice soon. You won't have to worry about seeing me anymore."

I wasn't sure how to react to the news, but I was curious by yet another shocking announcement from her. "Why are you quitting? Is it because of me?"

Claire released a slight chuckle. "No, Jill, it's not because of you. It takes a lot more for someone to make me run."

I suddenly had an alarming thought. "Wait! Are you pregnant?" I didn't wait for her to answer. Instead, I crossed my arms and narrowed my eyes. "That would explain the rushed wedding. You're pregnant, aren't you?"

Claire looked away for a moment; her cheeks blushed, and her eyes sad. "No, Jill, I'm not pregnant."

"So why the sad face, and why are you quitting?"

"I don't want to get into details, but Travis and I might go into business together, and I want to give it one hundred percent of my time."

I creased my brow again. "Business together. Doing what? Oh, wait. Are you doing another Slater and Sabela thing? Are you going to be doing that building stuff with Travis?"

"No, it's something else, and it may not even happen. But I want to give it my best shot."

I was dying to know. "So what is it? Why all the secrecy? You told me about you and Travis getting married, fearing I'd hear about it from someone else. Well, what makes you think I wouldn't hear about this from another source?" I gave her a canning grin, knowing I had her. She'd have to tell me now.

Claire rested her palms on the counter. "Look, I've probably already said too much. I'm sure Sabela will fill you in if it happens."

My face froze. "Sabela? What does she have to do with it? I've not seen her since we met for lunch the day after Travis broke up with me." I shook my head as I remembered that day. "God, I was a mess." I folded my arms again and leaned back in my chair. "Are you friends with her now? You stole my boyfriend, and now you've taken my friend. What else do you want, Claire?"

Claire raised her voice, catching me off guard. "For the last time, Jill, I didn't steal your boyfriend. Travis is still working for Slater, so yes, I have spoken to Sabela. I'm not stealing your friends, okay. I shouldn't have said anything. You think everyone is out to get you. That's not the case. Maybe one day, when you get off your high horse, we could be civil to each other and have a decent conversation without all the accusations. If that ever happens, I'd be happy to fill you in. Just let me know. Until then, I'm done. Have a nice day."

I was insulted by Claire's remarks, and watched as she raised her hands and stormed off. "Now, wait a minute. You can't just walk off and leave me hanging." I yelled.

Claire didn't look back. "Watch me." She hollered from across the room before disappearing behind the door that led to her little x-ray room.

The lobby fell silent, and I remained in my seat, stunned by what Claire had just told me. Not only was she marrying Travis, but they were also going into business together. It's obvious Sabela knows what is going on. I reached for my phone. Sabela always opened up to me about everything. Glancing down, I located her number and hit the call button.

# CHAPTER 2

*A*fter five rings, Sabela's phone went to voicemail. "Damn it," I whispered while the recorded message spoke. After the beep sounded, I said in my friendliest voice. "Hey Sabela, it's Jill. I haven't seen you in a while and thought we could catch up. I miss you. Call me. I'd love to have lunch with you soon. Bye." I ended the call feeling disappointed. I hated not knowing what Claire and Travis were up to. And how was Sabela involved?

I glanced at my phone, relieved to see it was almost lunchtime. I needed to get away from this place and get some fresh air. I texted Sadie, who has been my roommate, since Travis moved out. She also worked here as a dental assistant, and we always took our lunches together.

It was perfect timing how things had worked out. She began working here a week before Travis and I separated. She mentioned she was looking for a place to live. The rest is history. We get along great; she's thirty, a few years older than me. A few weeks ago, though, she met a guy at a bar where we had gone for a couple of drinks after work, and I think she has fallen pretty hard for him. His name is Logan. He builds surfboards and has a store close to the beach. I can't say I blame her; he's gorgeous. His body has a deep copper tan, which extenuates his shoulder-length hair naturally bleached by the sun.

Sadie and I had spotted him standing at the bar, looking our way. We nudged elbows and giggled, both drooling at the mouth. When he walked our way, I was sure he was coming to talk to me, but as he approached our table, I saw his eyes were fixed on Sadie. Sadie beamed at him with a huge smile. I suddenly found myself alone. Logan pulled up a chair across from Sadie, and the two were instantly mesmerized by each other. It was definitely a mutual attraction. I found myself consumed with jealousy. I wanted what she was experiencing right at that moment.

I felt foolish that I had assumed he liked me over Sadie. I always thought I was the prettiest between the two of us. Especially since I had dyed my hair blonde again after Travis left, I let it grow out a year ago, but it's back looking full and luscious, and I feel like the old me again. Flirtatious and pretty. Sadie is more relaxed and loves the cowboy look and country music. It's all she plays at home and in her car. I'm slowly taking a liking to it, but Madonna and Jennifer Lopez are more my styles.

That night she had worn her usual wardrobe, faded denim jeans, and a black t-shirt, dressed with a suede fringed vest and cowboy boots. She loved turquoise jewelry and wore plenty on her fingers and around her neck. But that night had been like any other night before Logan appeared.

We'd gone out in the past and hung out with guys in the bars that offered to buy us drinks. But that's as far as it went. We had no interest in going home with them. It was just some fun on a night out.

But this was different. I could see it in Sadie's and Logan's eyes. Their body language was a dead giveaway, too. They both leaned in towards each other. Their elbows rested on the table. If they leaned in a few more inches more, they'd be kissing.

Sadie had forgotten about me sitting next to her until Logan spoke, keeping his eyes on Sadie. "Can I buy you, ladies, a drink?" he asked.

Sadie turned to me; her eyes were bright. "Do you want a drink?"

I shook my head. I felt out of place. "Nah. I think I am going to go home. I'm pretty tired. Do you mind?" I had told her as I stood up.

Sadie's smile disappeared, and she took my hand. "Are you okay?"

"Yeah, I'm fine. I'll see you at home. Logan seems like a nice guy. So I'm sure you'll be fine."

Logan turned to me and smiled. "I promise to take real good care of her."

Sadie made it home safely that night. I had fallen asleep. But I noticed the bounce in her step as she skipped across the room to get her morning coffee the next day. Her smile was big, and her eyes were bright.

Still dressed in my bathrobe, I poured myself a cup of coffee and chuckled at Sadie. "Well, aren't we the happy one? I guess you and Logan hit it off."

Sadie leaned back in her chair at the table, where she now sat with her mug, laughing. "Oh my god, yes, we did. We had such a great time. He makes me laugh, and he can dance too. We got up a few times and danced to a few slow songs. But, man, I loved how he held my body close to his."

I felt my cheeks blush as Sadie described her newfound crush. I was slightly envious but happy for her.

Since that night, Sadie saw Logan numerous times and never came home on Saturday night. However, when she walked through the door Sunday morning, she had the face of a girl who just got laid. For the entire day, she did nothing but talk about Logan. Sadie and I had not been friends for long, but I have a feeling that what we have may suffer and become second to Sadie's new relationship with Logan.

Sadie finally texted me back and said Logan would join us for lunch. I didn't want to be the third wheel and told her to have fun, and I'd see her at home tonight. She replied with a simple okay. For the first time in months, it seemed I would spend my lunch alone. The decision I had now was—where? I didn't want to sit in a restaurant alone and opted to do a drive-thru and eat in my car at the park. The menu was limited for my choices, and I opted for a salad and an iced tea.

For the next thirty minutes, I sat in my car and picked at my salad while I felt sorry for myself. I wasn't used to being alone. I have had a boyfriend for the past four years and plenty of friends. Now it seemed they were all moving on with their lives, settling down and making life-changing choices. My life, on the other hand, remained the same, if not worse. I still worked the tedious job as a receptionist; I had no boyfriend or any close friends for that matter and no exciting plans for the future. The worst part about all of this was that I had to admit that I was jealous of Claire —not because she was marrying Travis. I'm definitely over him. It's because she had goals, and from what little she told me, it sounded like she had a bright future ahead. What do I have? I do the same job day in and day out, work out at the gym, and lately, since Sadie met Logan, I've spent my nights alone at home. I need to figure out what I want to do in life. I'm not getting any younger.

My phone dinged, interrupting my thoughts. I glanced down at the screen where the phone sat on the seat and saw Sabela had text me. I picked it up and read her message.

*Hey Jill, it's so good to hear from you. I'm so sorry I've not been in touch. So much has happened since I last saw you. I'll fill you in over lunch. I have a lot to tell you. So make it a long lunch. Tell me where and when you want to meet, and I'll be there. I gotta run. Bye.*

I threw the phone down on the seat in disgust. So a lot has happened in her life too. So when I see her for lunch I'm going to be sitting there listening to all her great news and of course she'll ask me what is new with me and I have nothing. So I wasn't in any mood to text her back and headed back to work.

When I pulled into the parking lot, I spotted Travis's truck, and then I saw Claire leaning in the driver's window. Travis's elbow peaked out where it leaned on the edge. "Well, just great. Now I have to witness these two lovebirds." I grunted under my breath. Claire was too busy leaning in the window, giggling and kissing Travis, to notice me. This was the first time I wished I didn't drive a hot pink mustang.

I eased my car slowly around to the side of the building, hoping they wouldn't notice me. They did not, and I quickly put the car in park and turned off the motor. The only way to enter the dentist's office was through the front door, directly in front of where Travis was parked. I glanced at my phone and saw I had a few minutes to spare before my hour was up and stayed in my car in the hopes Travis would soon leave.

Five minutes later, I heard the familiar sound of his truck fire up, and I watched with my head ducked down, which didn't matter; everyone knew my car. I watched with relief as Travis headed to the parking lot's exit and came to a stop to let oncoming traffic pass. The dentist was on a busy main road, and traffic was plentiful at this time of day.

I remained in my car, waiting until Travis had merged onto the busy street. I was afraid he would spot me in his rearview mirror. A few minutes passed, and I saw the traffic had slowed down. The light must have turned red at the intersection. I watched as Travis pulled out onto the main road and turned into the right lane.

A few seconds later, I screamed at the top of my lungs as I watched a black pickup truck come from nowhere at high speed and crash hard into Travis's truck. I covered my ears when the black truck impacted the driver-side door where Travis sat. It wasn't a tap; it was a hard hit with the force of speed behind it. The loud sound of the truck crashing into Travis's truck kept replaying in my head. It was deafening. "No!" I screamed at the loud screeching sound of brakes, and the smell of burning rubber from the skidding tires overpowered my senses. My hand gripped the door handle as I watched in horror. Travis's truck spun out of control across the highway. Other cars skidded to a stop, barely missing his vehicle as it slid to the other side and crashed into a street lamp, where it came to a sudden halt.

# CHAPTER 3

My heart raced and my chest heaved as I tried to catch my breath. "Oh my god!" I cried as I struggled with my car door, trying desperately to open it. I heard another loud crash, but where it came from was out of my view. I suddenly realized it must have been the truck that hit Travis. It must have crashed into something else. After he hit Travis, he disappeared out of my view.

I scrambled out of my car. My legs shook, and it took me a minute to steady myself. "Travis," I screamed as I raced towards his truck, oblivious to cars that slowed down to look, but continued to drive on. Then, in the middle of the highway, I saw some vehicles pulled over to the side of the road, exiting their cars. "Travis," I screamed again.

His truck wrapped around the pole. The entire driver's side was caved in, and from what I could tell, Travis was not moving from inside. I yelled his name again, with tears pouring down my cheeks. My body trembled, fearing what I might find. I heard a commotion to my right and scanned the street. The driver of the other truck was trying to get out of his vehicle. Two men were yelling at him, telling him to stay put until the cops arrived. They stood in the space of the open door, pushing him back, preventing him from leaving. I heard the man scream obscenities and tried to fight back. But the two men were much bigger and prevailed, keeping him at the scene.

When I reached Travis's truck, I brought my hand up to my mouth and gasped. "Oh my god!" His truck was a tangled mess of metal. I heard footsteps behind me and saw three men racing towards Travis's truck. "Help! Please help," I screamed. "He's not moving."

I turned away and looked inside the shattered window on the driver's side. I couldn't see anything. The spider web of broken glass shielded my view.

A middle-aged man approached me out of breath and rested his hand on my shoulder. "Do you know him?"

"He is my ex-boyfriend. We need to help him." I grabbed the door handle of the truck and pulled hard, using all my strength. "The door won't open. Oh god. We need to get him out of there."

I watched as my hands clenched together up to my face. The three men tried with all their strength to open the crushed door. But it was no use.

The man that had touched my shoulder tried to soothe my panicked state by using a calm tone when he spoke. "My friend here has called the cops. They will be here shortly. They will get him out."

Suddenly I heard a female voice scream, "Travis!" I spun my head around and saw Claire racing across the road. Unfortunately, she didn't look for oncoming traffic when she ran out. I held my breath and froze when I saw a car skid to a stop, barely missing her by inches. Claire raised her hand as she continued to run in my direction. I don't think she realized a car almost hit her. "Claire!" I cried with my arms open.

She didn't hesitate and sought the comfort of my embrace.

Now was not the time to be concerned about our differences. I wrapped my arms around her and consoled her shaking body.

"What happened?" she sobbed.

He was t-boned by the black truck across the street. The driver tried to leave, but those two guys standing next to him are making sure he doesn't."

Claire pulled away from my embrace and scanned the street. "Where's Travis?"

"He's still in the truck. The door won't open. It's jammed. The whole side is caved in."

Claire rushed to the door and tried to pull it open. "Oh my god. I can't see him." She screamed in a panic. "What about the passenger side?"

"That side is jammed up with the pole."

Claire looked up and down the street frantically. "Where are the friggin 'cops? We need help! He could be seriously injured."

My head spun around when I heard a loud thud and saw that a man came to help. He jumped onto the mangled hood of the truck and tried peering through the windshield. It was splashed with cracks and webs of shattered glass. "I can see him," he yelled.

Claire and I gasped and spoke the same words at the same time. "Is he moving?"

"Hold on." The guy said as he inched his face closer to the glass to get a better look. "No, he is not. His body is flopped over the steering wheel. He is not moving at all."

Suddenly I heard sirens off in the distance. "The cops are coming. I can hear the sirens." I bellowed. "They will be here soon."

Claire put her face to the window on the driver's side. "Travis! Travis! Can you hear me?" She screamed. "Please, Travis, wake up." She turned to me with tears pouring down her cheeks. "I can't see or hear anything. He's not moving. Why isn't he moving?"

She fell into my arms, and I held her tight. My tears were just as plentiful as hers." I don't know why he is not moving Claire. I hear the sirens getting closer. I think they are on the next block." I looked over her shoulder and down the street and saw the flashing red lights. "Yes. Here they come."

Claire raised her head and looked toward where the sound of the sirens was coming from. "I see a fire truck and ambulance too," she said, pulling herself away and tried one more time to open the driver's side door. "Damn it!" she screamed.

The man that had climbed on the hood jumped down onto the ground and approached me. "The fireman will get him out. My friends and I will stay in case they need any help."

I nodded. "Thank you."

Within a few minutes, three patrol cars, a fire truck, and an ambulance surrounded us. All came to an abrupt halt behind Travis's truck.

Across the street, spectators had exited their buildings and looked on. Cars had pulled over and sat idly watching the accident scene. Then, a patrol car had finally stopped in the far lane with its flashing amber lights left on to block the road closest to Travis's truck. Two police officers exited the vehicle. One was talking on his radio as they approached us. A fire truck and an ambulance parked directly behind the patrol car, and without a second to waste, the firemen hastily jumped down into the road and ran over to Travis's truck. "What do we have here?" One fireman yelled.

Claire swept her hair out of her face and wiped her moist cheeks. "My fiancée is in that truck. We can't get the doors open, and he is not moving." She cried.

I looked across the street and saw the other two officers were in the man's truck that hit Travis.

"Can anyone tell me what happened?" an officer asked, standing next to us.

"I can. I saw the whole thing?" I answered. My voice trembled when I spoke.

"And you are?" the officer asked.

"Jill. My name is Jill Anderson. I am Travis's—the guy stuck in the truck. I am his ex-girlfriend." The officer glanced over at Claire. "And you are his fiancée. Correct?"

Claire nodded. "Yes."

I looked over at Travis's truck, where six firemen now surrounded it. Two on the hood, two at the driver's side door, and two in the bed. They were all trying to figure out a way to free Travis.

"Jill, can you tell me what happened?" The officer asked.

I turned my attention away from the firemen to face the officer. "Yes, I was sitting in that parking lot across the street." I pointed toward my work. "I worked there and had just got back from lunch. Travis was leaving, and when he pulled out into the road, that black truck over there." I pointed again. "Came from nowhere and slammed into him."

The officer nodded and turned to Claire. "Did you see anything?"

Claire shook her head. "No, I was inside. I had just said goodbye to Travis. I heard the crash and came running out. I didn't see it happen."

The officer nodded. "How old is your fiancée, ma'am?" the officer asked.

"He is thirty."

"And what does he do for a living?

"He is in construction," Claire replied.

"So I'm assuming he is in pretty good shape to be in that line of work?"

"Yes, he is, officer," Claire replied as she glanced over at the firemen crawling and climbing over Travis's truck. "How are they going to get him out of there?"

"Your fiancée is in good hands. They will have him out soon, I promise. When they do, I need you, two ladies, to stand back and let the men do their work."

Claire and I both nodded and turned to watch the crew attempt to free Travis. I am taller than Claire by a good six inches and wrapped my arm around her shoulder as she sobbed some more and rested her head on my chest.

"He has to be okay." Claire cried as she sniffed back her tears.

"Shh, I'm sure he will be." I said, unable to stop my voice from trembling. I pleaded in my head for Travis's life to be saved. He was too young to die, and I suddenly thought of his and Claire's future. They were just starting out. They had their whole lives ahead of them. I wiped my eyes with my free hand when I thought about their upcoming wedding. Why did it take this accident to make me realize that Claire and Travis had so much more than Travis and I ever had? I realized then that I was okay with their relationship. Travis finally got what he wanted—the real deal. Towards the end of our relationship, he had said he wanted the real deal, but that we weren't it. He was right.

Whatever I felt before the accident had disappeared entirely. Whether it was anger or jealousy, I'm not really sure. Instead, I now accepted that Travis and Claire were a couple, and I wanted nothing more than Travis to recover and begin his life with Claire. My heart ached for her. I was feeling her pain. There was once a time I had loved Travis like she does, and I can only imagine the hurt she is going through. I want to be there for her. Comfort her and show her I do have feelings. Something I never did with Travis. But will she let me after the way I have treated her?

Snapping myself out of my life-changing thoughts, I heard the loud shatter of glass and gasped. Claire raised her head and grabbed my hand. She held it tight as she stared at the scene with wide eyes. It was almost like she was watching a horror movie. "Travis!" she screamed.

"Shh, Claire," I whispered.

One fireman shattered the driver's side window and pulled the glass out of the frame in pieces, and let the glass drop to the ground. "Travis, can you hear me?" The fireman yelled. Travis did not move or reply.

I could see Travis's limp body hunched over the steering wheel from where we stood. "Come on, Travis. Move. Say something." I ushered in a panicked voice.

"Travis, can you hear me?" The fireman yelled again as he removed the last piece of glass. He turned to the fireman that was standing next to him and shook his head. "No response. Let's try to get this door open." He ordered.

The other firemen climbed off the truck and went to assist. Using crowbars and a lot of muscle, they forced the door open just enough so they could reach Travis. I turned my head when I heard the running of feet and saw the two ambulance men pull up alongside the truck with a gurney on wheels. One fireman reached in and dragged Travis's body back off the wheel. And that was when I saw the blood smeared across his face.

"Oh my god, he is bleeding." I cried. "His face is covered in blood."

Claire gasped and held her hands up to her mouth. "Oh my god. Why isn't he moving?"

With my body tense and my heart racing, I watched as two of the firemen gently pulled Travis's lifeless body out of the truck and onto the gurney. The ambulance men shared a few words with the firemen and raced him off to the ambulance.

"Can I ride with him in the ambulance?" Claire pleaded with the officer.

"They have to stabilize him and check all his vitals. They are taking him to San Diego hospital. If you want to head over there in your car, you can." The officer replied, turning away to talk on his radio.

"You can ride with me, Claire. I want to go too."

She grasped my hands together with hers and closed her eyes for a moment. "Thank you."

"I'll call work on the way. Unfortunately, Dr. Larson will have to do without us for the rest of the day." I looked up and saw one of the men that had stayed behind to help was approaching us.

"Is he going to be okay?" he asked.

I shook my head. "We don't know. He isn't moving or responding. We are going to go to the hospital and wait. Thank you so much for your help."

"It's no problem. I hope he is going to be okay. Good luck, okay."

"Thank you."

After the man left with his friends, I ushered Claire across the street to my car, whispering under my breath. "Please don't die, Travis; Claire needs you." Then, I paused and closed my eyes, "And I need you as a friend."

# CHAPTER 4

laire and I watched from the curb as the two men raced to the ambulance and loaded Travis inside. One of the ambulance men remained in the back with Travis while the other ran to the driver's side, jumped in, and sped off with the red light flashing and the sirens blasting.

I took Claire's hand and ran across the street to my car. "Come on, let's go," I said, as my chest pounded. Claire gripped my hand tight and raced across the street with me. Neither one of us paid attention to any oncoming cars and was thankful for the ones that slowed down to let us cross.

We reached my car out of breath and gasping for air, but neither one of us wanted to wait the extra seconds it would take to catch our breath. I had left my car unlocked with the door wide open and was just about to jump in when I heard a male voice call my name.

"Jill, where are you going?"

I turned my head and saw Doctor Larson standing in front of the dental office. "It's Travis. He was in that truck that got hit. We have to go to the hospital."

I rolled my eyes when he walked to my car. "Oh, my goodness. Is he okay?"

I didn't want to stand around and chitchat. "We don't know. He wasn't moving when they pulled him out. They took him straight to the hospital. We have to go there. I'm not sure if you are aware, but Travis and I broke up a few months ago. He is engaged to Claire now." I saw the look of surprise on his face. "It's a long story. I will fill you in later, but we really have to go. I'm sorry."

Doctor Larson raised his hand. "No, it's fine. Please call me when you have a chance and let me know how he is doing. Sadie is here; we will manage."

"Thank you," I replied. Then, before he had any more questions, I quickly jumped in my car and started the engine.

As I pulled up to merge onto the road, the horrific accident I had just witnessed less than an hour ago replayed in my mind. I was idling in my car in the same spot where Travis was when it happened. I glanced across the street as I visioned Travis making an impact with the pole a second time. Again, the deafening sounds and my screams played in my head.

With caution, I pulled out onto the main road and headed towards the hospital. I glanced over at Claire. She had her elbow resting on the window ledge, and her hand supported her head. She was crying, and I cried for her and Travis. "We will be there soon, okay," I said in a soothing tone through my tears.

She nodded as tears rolled down her cheeks. "I can't lose him, Jill. I'm so scared."

I reached over and rested my hand on her shoulder. "Travis is a strong man. He's going to be okay."

Claire shook her head and rocked in her seat. "We don't know that, Jill. He wasn't moving, and he had all that blood over his face. Did it dawn on you that his airbags didn't deploy? I didn't see any of them."

It hadn't struck me until she had mentioned it. "You're right; they didn't. Why is that? He must have hit that steering wheel hard when the other guy crashed into him. No wonder he was bleeding."

"Maybe because he wasn't moving fast. You said he was just pulling out of the parking lot, so he must have been going pretty slow." Claire flopped back in her seat. "God, I don't know. I feel like I'm living a nightmare." She glanced out of the window. "Are we almost there?"

"Another five minutes," I replied while driving faster than the speed limit and dodging traffic. I ignored the car horns as I raced by and released a heavy breath when I changed lanes without colliding or hitting someone.

"Slow down, Jill. We don't need another accident." Claire shrieked as I narrowly missed hitting a white Honda.

I looked down at my speedometer and saw I was driving sixty in a thirty-five-mile zone. I tapped on the brakes. "Shit, I'm sorry. I just want to get to Travis."

Claire rolled her eyes. "Me too. But alive," she stressed as she wiped her moist cheeks.

A few minutes later, we were pulling into the busy parking lot of the hospital. "Shit, this place is packed." I barked. "Where am I supposed to park?" I complained as I drove down the endless rows.

"There's a spot." Claire suddenly blasted with her finger, pointing to an empty space.

I quickly pulled in and turned off the car. "Are you ready?" I asked Claire, who gazed at the tall hospital building.

"He's somewhere in that building," Claire said softly while still staring out of the window. "Do you think he is alive?"

"I'm trying to stay positive and believe that he is," I said, matching her soft tone. "You have to believe that too, Claire."

She turned to face me. Her glassy eyes couldn't hide the fear she was feeling. "I won't be able to live without him. What if he isn't?"

I reached over and took her hand. "Whatever the outcome is, we will get through this together. We may have started off on the wrong foot, and I'm sorry for that. But I can tell you; I am here for you."

Claire gave me a weak smile. "Thank you." She released a heavy sigh. "I'm ready."

I nodded. "Okay then. Let's go."

# CHAPTER 5

Our blood was pumping through our veins at high gear as we raced through the parking lot to the hospital's main building. When we reached the front double glass doors, I held onto the metal handle as I sucked in oxygen to catch my breath. Claire did the same.

"Okay, come on. Let's see if we can get some information at the front desk."

Still out of breath, Claire nodded and followed my lead. The front desk was off to the left and well-lit. A young red-headed receptionist sat behind the desk, staring at a computer monitor. When we approached, she looked up. "Can I help you?"

I rested my elbows on the cool marble surface. "Yes, my friend's fiancée was in a terrible car accident, and they brought him here."

"He wasn't moving." Claire shrieked.

I turned to Claire and grabbed her upper arm. "Shh, Claire. Let me talk."

"I'm sorry. I just need to know if he is going to be okay."

The nurse gave us a caring smile. "I understand. What is his name?"

"Travis Trent," I replied. "It's only been thirty minutes since the ambulance left."

The nurse tapped some entries into her computer and waited for it to load. She shook her head. "I don't have any updated information yet. He's being admitted for being unresponsive at the scene of an accident and trauma to the head."

"Yes, that's right," Claire cried. "Does it say if he is responding?"

The nurse shook her head. "I have no updates yet. I will let them know the family is here, and a doctor will come out and talk to you shortly. Why don't you have a seat in the waiting area?"

I scanned the area behind us and saw a waiting area off to the right. Come on, Claire, it's right over here." I told her as I took her arm and guided her to the row of seats. Claire sat down first and immediately cried again. "Why can't they tell us anything?"

The seating area was quiet, with only another couple sitting three rows behind us against the wall. I gave them a subtle smile and took a seat next to Claire. "They are probably still assessing him. I'm sure it will take a while."

Claire sat up straight and rubbed her eyes on her sweatshirt. "I'll stay here all night if I have to."

"And I will too. I'm not going anywhere, Claire."

Claire raked her hands through her short hair and pulled back her bangs. "Jill, why are you being so nice to me? We've hardly shared two words since I started dating Travis, and when I told you we were engaged, I thought you were going to rip my head off."

I released a slight chuckle. "You are right. We've never been what you could call buddies, and yes, I'm not going to deny it. I've been angry ever since Travis came into work and announced he was seeing you." I chuckled again. "I despised you, and I hate to admit it, but I hated Travis after he had told me. But at the same time, I was jealous of the two of you. I wanted what you had. I could see the love seeping out of Travis's eyes when he looked at you. He never looked at me that way."

"I'm sorry, Jill. We didn't mean to hurt you." Claire shrugged her shoulders. "It just happened."

"I know that now. But I couldn't see beyond my rage, and when you told me you were engaged, I was more jealous than angry because Travis had never asked me to marry him." I turned to Claire and gave her a weak smile. "But none of that matters anymore. Whatever anger or jealousy I was feeling, I don't feel it anymore." A tear trickled down my face, and I gently wiped it away. "I'm embarrassed to say it, but it took Travis's accident to make me realize how childish I have been."

Claire sensed my remorse and took my hand. "It's okay, Jill. So much has happened in the last few months. I don't hold anything against you. If I were in your shoes, I would have probably acted the same way." Claire paused for a minute. "I'm sure you had mixed feelings for Travis at the time."

I nodded. "I don't know what I was feeling. The last few months with him were horrible. We did nothing but fight. I guess I just didn't want to admit that it was over. But that is no excuse for the way I treated you. I'm truly sorry. Please forgive me."

Claire showed me a weak smile and squeezed my hand. "I do, and thank you for being here."

"Please don't thank me. I thought I hated Travis after we broke up, but I could never hate him. We had a few good years before things went sour. I'm happy for the two of you and would like us all to be friends if that is possible."

"I would like that. And I know Travis will too." Claire looked down the hallway, past the front desk. "God, where is the doctor? What is taking them so long?"

"Let me go ask the receptionist again." I'll be right back."

I saw the tears pooling in Claire's eyes again when she nodded in silence, and I embraced her before standing. The receptionist smiled as I approached her. "Any news?"

She shook her head. "Nothing yet. I'm sorry. I'm sure they will be along soon. There is a cafeteria down the hall if you want to grab a coffee."

The thought of anything entering my stomach made my insides churn. "No, we are good, thanks. We don't want to miss the doctor."

Claire looked at me with hope in her eyes. "Did she tell you anything"

"No. But she thinks someone will be here soon. I'm going to use the restroom. I'll be right back."

Relieved to find the restroom empty, I stood at the sink and glanced at the unfamiliar reflection in the mirror. My makeup was non-existent, and my blonde hair was uncombed and tangled. This morning I wouldn't have dreamt of being seen in public in such a state. I would have been in here reapplying my makeup and making sure every hair was in place. For the first time, I didn't care. It seemed so trivial after what happened to Travis, and then suddenly it hit me, and I screamed. "Travis, you have to be okay! You have so much to live for." I gripped the edge of the white porcelain sink with both hands until my knuckles turned white and leaned in until I was just inches away from the mirror. I talked to my reflection and prayed—something I had not done since I went to church with my mom and dad as a child. "Please, God. I'm begging you to please let Travis live. Please don't take him away from us yet. Claire needs him. I need him." I closed my eyes. "God, I am begging you. Please help Travis." I cried as I raked my fingers through my hair before giving it a vigorous shake. "Okay, pull yourself together, Jill. You need to get back out there and be strong for Claire."

When I returned, I found Claire crying hysterically into her phone.

"I promise I will call as soon as I know something. Thank you, Slater. I'll see you soon." Claire cried and then ended the call.

"Slater called you?"

Claire shook her head and wiped her eyes. "No, I called him.

Travis was on his way back to work when he had the accident. I'm sure Slater was probably wondering where he was. He's going to pick up Sabela, and they are going to come over here."

Now was not the time to pry about her friendship with Sabela, I told myself. The last I remembered, Sabela always had a grudge with her; because of what Claire's brother, Davin, had done. I thought back to that time and still can't believe he had tried to rape her because she wouldn't move to Texas with him. I guess Claire was right. A lot has happened over the past few months.

Claire held her phone to her chest while she spoke. "I called my mom and dad, too. They are on their way over."

I nodded. "I haven't seen Sabela since Travis and I broke up."

"They have a son now. His name is Scottie."

My jaw dropped. "What. I saw Sabela a few months ago. How can that be? She wasn't pregnant. I'm sure of it. Unless she had a tiny baby."

Claire released a small laugh. "No, she didn't have the baby. It's Slaters. He and Eve had a son, but Eve left him and never told him about Scottie. It's a long story. I'm sure they will fill you in on everything, but it's not my place to tell you. I may have said too much as it is."

"Wow. Are you sure it's only been a few months? I can't believe all the shit that has happened." We were interrupted by what seemed to be a doctor dressed in white attire coming through the double doors. My heart raced, and my palms sweaty as I watched him walk towards us. Claire took my hand and squeezed it tight before we stood to our feet and waited for the news.

He was middle-aged and quite attractive, with his dark wavy hair and tanned skin. I zoned in on his left hand and noticed the wedding band. I immediately cast him off.

"Good afternoon. I am doctor Ryan."

Claire gave him a shy smile. "I am Travis's fiancée."

I butted in, "And I am his ex."

The doctors gave us the familiar confused look like Dr. Larson had given us and the police.

He turned his attention to Claire, who pleaded with the doctor for some good news. "Is he still alive? Please tell me he is a doctor."

Doctor Ryan gave her a weak smile. "He is alive, yes."

Claire grabbed her chest as her legs gave in, and she collapsed into a chair behind her. "Oh, thank god."

Unable to remain standing, I, too, felt weak in my legs. I fell into the seat next to Claire. "Thank god he is alive." I wept as tears pooled in my eyes.

Claire raised her head to Doctor Ryan. "When can we see him?"

The smile disappeared from his face, and he took a seat next to Claire. "He is alive, but I'm afraid he is in a coma."

# CHAPTER 6

Claire couldn't hide her fear and gasped. "Oh my god, no. Is he going to wake up?"

I reached over and took Claire's hand. "I can't believe this."

Doctor Ryan whispered. "I'm sorry I cannot predict a time frame for his recovery. Travis has suffered a severe head injury. Every injury is different."

Claire repeated her question. "But will he wake up?"

The doctor's smile returned, followed by a slight nod. "I believe he will. It's just a matter of time. The CT scan showed some swelling in the brain. Once the swelling has gone down, he should resume consciousness. Now he has no other injuries except for some bruising on the face from when he hit the steering wheel and a broken nose."

Claire hesitated before she spoke. "Will he have any side effects from the coma?"

"We won't know until he is awake. He is being transferred to the ICU ward, where they will put him on a ventilator and a feeding tube. We will monitor him closely, and all we can do is wait."

Claire gasped again. "The ICU?"

"Can we see him?" I asked.

The doctor glanced my way and nodded. "Yes, you can see him once he is settled and after we have run a few more tests."

"When will that be?" Claire asked anxiously.

"Not for a few hours. The cafeteria is open if you want to get something to eat. A nurse will come and get you when you can see him," Doctor Ryan told her.

Claire shook her head. "No. I can't eat anything right now."

Doctor Ryan saw the worry seeping from Claire's eyes and spoke softly. "I know this is difficult for you, but you have to be strong for Travis. I suggest you talk to him just like you do every day when you see him. Act naturally around him. Let him hear your happy voices. He may be unconscious, but he might be able to hear you, and it may help him wake up."

"Thank you; we will," Claire replied, turning to face me. "What do we talk to him about?"

Doctor Ryan overheard and answered her question. "Don't overthink it. Be natural. Tell him about your day and what you are having for dinner. Talk about work and life at home. Do you have children? You could talk about them."

"No, we don't, doctor, but we have a dog. Her name is Tilly."

Doctor Ryan beamed at her with a big smile. "There you go. You can tell him how Tilly is doing."

"That's a good idea. He loves Tilly. We've only been together a few months, but they bonded like glue."

Doctor Ryan glanced my way. "He was with you before then?"

I nodded. "Yes, we were together for four years. It's a long story." I waved the subject off with my hands. I felt like an old record.

"I'm sure it is," Doctor Ryan replied. "Well, it's great you can all be friends. But, listen, I need to get back. A nurse will come when Travis is ready, and I will be here for questions you may have, and I will be talking to you every day."

Claire shook his hand. "Thank you, doctor."

I extended my hand. Doctor Ryan took it and gave it a gentle shake. "Thank you," I said with a weak smile.

After doctor Ryan had left, I turned to Claire. "Are you sure you don't want anything to eat?"

"No. I'm good. Slater and Sabela should be here soon. I don't want to miss them."

"You are right. I forgot."

Claire released a heavy sigh. "God, I can't believe he is in a coma. Can't people be in comas for years?"

She was right, but not wanting to scare her; I downplayed it. "Yeah, I guess if they have really bad injuries. But, from what the doctor told us, just some swelling needs to go down, and then he should wake up."

Claire leaned back and closed her eyes. "Oh, I hope so. If he is in a coma for a long time, he may wake up like a vegetable. He will have to learn to do everything we take for granted all over again, like walking, eating, and talking. Oh, Travis, why did this happen to you? Why you?"

I leaned in and rested my hand on her shoulder. "Hey now. Don't make any assumptions. We don't know that. The only thing we can do is hope that Travis pulls out of this and makes a full recovery."

"Yeah, I know, but I'm so scared. So many what-ifs are going through my head? I can't just shut them off. I've never known anyone that has been in a coma. I don't know what to do or what to expect."

"I hear you. I'm trying hard not to lose it. It's like we are living in a nightmare. I want it to end. I want to wake up. This can't be happening."

The voice of a man echoed through the lobby. "Claire. Jill."

Claire and I turned our heads at the same time—startled to hear our names and saw Slater and Sabela running towards us.

I released a deep breath—relieved to see them and jumped to my feet. "Oh, thank god. They are here."

Claire stood when she saw them but was unable to speak. But then, something triggered her emotions again, and she could only stand and weep.

Sabela raced to her and took her in her arms. "Oh, Claire. I'm so sorry. Have you heard anything?" But Claire could not answer. Instead, her tears increased to heart-wrenching sobs.

Slater turned to me and opened his arms. Without hesitation, I collapsed into them and cried for Travis. "Jill, I didn't know you were going to be here," Slater said, rubbing my back to soothe me.

I pulled away and stared into his eyes as I replayed the horrific accident once again in my head—a horrible memory that would stay with me for the rest of my life. Finally, I spoke through my endless tears. "I saw it happen, Slater."

Slater's eyes grew wide as he looked at me with a furrowed brow. "What? Where were you?"

I was in the parking lot. I was just about to go back to work after lunch. Travis had just dropped off Claire, and when he pulled out onto the main road, another truck came from nowhere and slammed into the driver's side of Travis's truck. He was driving fast and struck Travis, and I watched as Travis spun out of control and crashed on the other side of the street, and now he is in a coma."

Sabela relaxed the hold she had on Claire. "He's in a coma?"

Claire wiped the tears from her cheeks before she spoke. "Yes, the doctor just came out and told us. He said we wouldn't be able to see him for a few more hours." Claire collapsed into Sabela's arms again. "I'm so glad you are here."

Sablela and Slater glanced at each other, unable to hide their shock while holding onto Claire and me. "My God, I can't believe this," Slater said. His voice was flat. "I need to sit down." He released the hold he had on me, and I noticed how unsteady he was on his feet and guided him to the chair close by.

"Do you want me to get you some water?" Sabela said as she took a seat next to him and held his hand.

"Yeah. If you don't mind."

"The cafeteria is open. I'll go with you." I replied. I was anxious to stretch my legs and take a walk somewhere. "Slater can stay with Claire."

"Okay, sounds good," Sabela said as she patted Slater's knee and rose to her feet. 'We won't be long. Do you want anything else?"

Slater shook his head. "No." He turned to Claire, who was now sitting next to him on his other side. "How about you, Claire? Do you want some water?"

"Yeah, I'll take a bottle."

When Sabela and I were alone in the long corridor that led to the cafeteria, we talked. "I'm sorry I've not been in touch since Travis and I broke up, but it's been a rough few months," I told her.

Sabela smiled. "It's okay. Slater and I have had a lot going on too. Did you hear Slater discovered he is a dad, and we are now raising his son? His name is Scottie." She beamed a big smile. "Oh, wait until you see him."

"Yeah, Claire mentioned something. I can't believe you are a mom. Where is he?"

"He is spending the night at his grandmother's, Patricia. Eve's mother. We called her and told her what had happened, and she met us halfway to pick up Scottie." Sabela paused. "So you and Claire are okay now?"

"I think so. Sadly, it was Travis's accident that brought us together. I can't believe how childish I have been acting. I feel terrible. I honestly want to make it up to Claire for the way I have treated her. And this might sound strange. I want to make it up to Travis, too. And before you get the wrong idea. I'm not looking to try to win Travis back. I just want him as a friend. I never realized how much I cared for him. I'd be devastated if he doesn't recover from all of this."

We were almost at the cafeteria, and Sabela stopped walking

and turned to face me. "I admire you, Jill. You've changed. What you just said was beautiful." Sabela released a slight chuckle. "I never thought you had it in you."

I raised my brow. "What's that supposed to mean?"

"Oh, come on, Jill. Don't play innocent with me." She cracked me a smile. "You've always been about Jill and nobody else." She nudged my elbow. "Am I right?"

I rolled my eyes and gave her a smile of defeat. "Yeah, I guess you are. "I have been a bit self-absorbent."

"A bit? How about a lot? This is great. You have come full circle. I'm proud of you."

"Thanks. It just sucks that it took Travis to get almost killed to realize how selfish I have been."

Sabela draped an arm over my shoulder. "Hey, don't be so hard on yourself. You've been through a lot in the past few hours. Don't try to sort it all out right now. Let's be here for Travis and Claire. They need us."

"You're right—enough about me. Speaking of Claire, when did you two become friends? We both avoided her like the plague. I did it because I had nothing in common with her. Or so I thought. I never attempted to get to know her. She's actually really nice. And you never talked to her because of Davin, right?"

"Yeah, that had a lot to do with it. I was blaming her for Davin's crime, which was wrong. But Travis pointed that out to me when he told Slater and me he was seeing her."

"Was that after Travis and I had broken up?"

"It was the last time I had lunch with you. When I returned home, Travis was there, having a beer with Slater. He had left you the night before after putting it off for months."

"Wait, did you know he was seeing Claire before he told me?"

I saw the guilt in her eyes before she spoke. "Yes, I did, and I kept telling Travis that he needed to tell you, but he was too afraid."

My jaw dropped, and I pulled away from Sabela. "Then why the hell didn't you tell me? I thought you were my friend."

Sabela reached out her hand, and I pulled away. "I am your friend, which is why I chose not to tell you. It wasn't my place to tell you Jill. I wasn't about to do Travis's dirty work. And why are we talking about this now? The man is fighting for his life while we stand here arguing about who should have told you about Claire."

"Because my feelings are hurt, and I feel like such a fool. Everyone knew about Claire but me."

"Oh, come on, Jill. Now is not the time. A few minutes ago, you just told me how you have changed, and you are okay with Claire and Travis being a couple."

"I am okay with it, but I'm not okay with you hiding stuff from me. What else have you been hiding?"

"Now you are just being ridiculous. I was looking out for you. That's why I didn't say anything. Now can we just drop this? I care about you, and since Travis and Claire have been dating, Claire and I have become friends. You were right when you said she is nice. I would like it if we could all be friends."

"I would like that too, but I'm shocked that you never told me. You of all people. I didn't know you were capable of holding a secret for so long."

"It wasn't long, Jill. Just a few months." Sabela raised her hands. "And I can't believe we are still having this conversation. Can we please just drop it?"

I rolled my eyes and folded my arms. "Fine. But I still think it was wrong of you not to tell me."

"Look, I'm sorry. Okay. If that is what you want. An apology. Now there are no more secrets. Let's just put all this behind us. Travis needs us to all get along."

"You're right. I'm sorry too. Let's get the water and head back. Slater and Claire are probably wondering where we are."

When we returned to the waiting area, we found Claire

huddled in the arms of who I assumed were her parents. Finally, Claire raised her head and freed herself from her mother's arms. "Mom, these are my friends Sabela and Jill."

Claire's mom wiped her eyes. "Hello, I'm Abigail, and this is my husband, Jeffery."

Sabela and I reached out and shook their hands.

"They can't stay long. Dad has a doctor's appointment in an hour. He had a heart attack no so long ago, so it's important they go even though he wanted to cancel. They will come back after their appointment." Claire told us as she held her mother's hand.

"I agree with Claire," I told them. "There is nothing you can do here except wait out here with us. No one can see him right now."

"I know that is what Claire told us." Abigail agreed.

Slater, who was sitting on the chair, hung up his phone.

"Who was on the phone?" Sabela asked.

"Ricky. I filled him in on Travis. He was out on a job, but he'll be heading over here soon. I told him to take the rest of the day off. You know I'm going to need him a lot while Travis recovers. I wonder if he needs the extra work?" he told Sabela.

"Whose Ricky?"

"He is one of the guys that works for me. I've known him since Sabela, and I started dating." Slater shook his head and chuckled. "Man, has he changed. He worked with us on a job in some condo when I worked for Drew. Man, he was just a shy little kid that saw Sabela and me getting it on. We embarrassed the shit out of him. He couldn't look us in the eyes after that."

Sabela laughed. "Oh, I remember. But now he is all buffed out from lifting weights, and I must say he's pretty hot."

Slater grinned. "Really. You never told me you thought he was hot."

Sabela tossed back her hair. "You don't need me to tell you. You've seen him. If you were a girl, you would say the same thing."

"Wow, I have been out of the loop. I need to meet this Ricky guy." I joked. But on the inside, I wasn't kidding. I was intrigued.

Fatigue set in. I felt drained from the emotions of the day and the trauma from witnessing the accident, which kept playing in my head. I had no idea what time it was and glanced out at the large windows behind us. The skies were fading to a shade of grey, and the trees were turning into shadows. The sun was setting, telling me it was dusk. Slater and Sabela were talking amongst themselves. Claire fell asleep after her parents returned for a while, but they left to go home. I leaned back in my chair and allowed my eyes to close.

A strange male voice close by woke me up. My eyes flickered as I tried to focus on them and saw Slater talking to a fine specimen of a man. I remained quiet as I studied him. He was tall. At least six feet and wore loose grey sweatpants and a white t-shirt that hugged his prominent abs, accentuating his broad, muscular arms. His body was lean without an ounce of fat. My eyes traveled up to his face framed by his shoulder-length wavy blonde hair that I'm sure had been highlighted. His cheekbones were high, and his eyes were bright. I think they were blue. Slater told him that no one had seen Travis yet, but stopped when he noticed I was awake.

"Hey, Jill. This is Ricky. I don't believe you have met."

I rose from my chair and held out my hand. Ricky turned to face me and gave me a warm smile that tickled my heart. When he took my hand in his and curled his fingers over mine, I was surprised at how warm his skin was. He shook my hand gently and cupped our entwined hands with his other one. "Hi, Jill. I've heard a lot about you. I'm surprised we've never met."

I found myself lost in his brilliant blue eyes. He was the perfect specimen of the male speeches. "I've not been around much since Travis and I broke up. It's been a rough few months." I confessed.

Ricky released my hand, and I felt the need to rub my sweaty palms on my black pants.

"Well, I wished we had met under better circumstances."

I lowered my head. Guilt was consuming me for feeling attracted to him when Travis fought for his life in a room somewhere in the same building. I glanced over at the empty seats. "Hey, where did Sabela and Claire go?"

"To the bathroom," Slater replied. They should be back soon. "How are you feeling?" Slater asked me.

"Okay, I guess. How long was I asleep for?"

"About half-an-hour." Here comes Claire and Sabela now."

"Has the doctor come out yet?" Claire asked when she approached us.

Slater shook his head. "No. No one has been here."

Claire rolled her eyes. "What is taking them so long? We have been here for hours."

No sooner had she spoken than we all turned our heads when we heard the double doors open and watched as Dr. Ryan walked towards us.

Claire spoke first. "Any news, doctor? Can we see him?"

Doctor Ryan gave her a caring smile. "He is comfortable now in the ICU. The tests didn't reveal any more injuries. However, he is still in a coma, and yes, you can see him."

Claire locked her hands and raised them to her mouth. "Oh, my god. Thank you."

"I think it would be better if you go into groups." Dr. Ryan suggested.

Claire turned and faced me. "Will you go with me?"

"Of course, and then Sabela, Slater, and Ricky can go after us." I wrapped my arm over Claire's shoulder. "Are you ready?"

# CHAPTER 7

Claire and I didn't speak much as we followed Dr. Ryan down the polished hallways of the hospital. Unsure of what to expect when we walked into Travis's room, I was lost in my thoughts of fearing the unknown, and I believed Claire was, too.

After many left and right turns and a ride in an elevator, Dr. Ryan stopped at the door to Travis's room. "Now remember. Try to act calm and natural. As I said, I'm uncertain, but he may be able to hear you."

We both nodded as he opened the door and entered the room. Claire and I followed closely behind him. The shades were drawn, and a small overhead light illuminated the room. Soft music played from the TV above on the wall. The beeping of the machines hooked up to Travis echoed around us.

"Oh, Travis." Claire cried in a whisper as she strolled to the side of his bed and gently took his hand.

Travis was unrecognizable as he lay motionless in the bed, being kept alive by a feeding tube, IV, and a breathing machine. My heart shattered at what I saw. His face was swollen on one side, with a large gash extended down his left cheek. His eyes, closed, were black and blue, and his lips sliced and cut in several places with swelling around his chin and upper lip. His head was bandaged. I wondered if he felt any pain or did the coma free him from that? I echoed Claire's words, "Oh, Travis."

"I'm going to leave you alone with him for a while." Doctor Ryan said. "If you need anything, the red button on the wall will call a nurse if you notice any kind of movement—a flutter of the eyes. Fingers or toes twitching, let us know immediately. He might be coming out of his coma."

Claire wiped her watery eyes and nodded. "We will, doctor, and thank you."

After doctor Ryan left, I approached the bed on the other side and took Travis's other hand. It was cool to the touch and lifeless. Claire had his hand up to her cheek, and my heart tore as I watched her sob and kissed the palm of his hand.

"Travis, it's Claire. I'm here, baby. Please come back to us. Jill is here, and Sabela and Slater are waiting to see you. Ricky is here, too. We all miss you so much."

I remained quiet while Claire poured her heart out, stunned by what I was seeing. I couldn't believe Travis was in a coma. A few hours ago, he was full of life, and newly engaged, now he laid oblivious to anything around him as he fought for his life.

"I know Tilly misses you, too. I haven't been home yet. I came straight here with Jill when I found out about the accident." Claire looked up and smiled. "You brought us together, Travis. Jill is here with me, and she cares about you so much."

I gave his hand a gentle squeeze. "I do, Travis. I'm so sorry about everything. Claire needs you. I know you will wake up soon. You just need your rest right now. Until you do, I promise I will take good care of Claire and help her in any way I can until you are able to. I'm just now finding out what an amazing woman she is. I am truly happy for the two of you, Travis. You really have found the love of your life, and one day I will find mine."

Claire stood up and brushed her fingers gently across Travis's forehead. "He looks so peaceful." She leaned in and gently rested her lips on his brow as tears streamed down her face. "I love you so much, Travis. Please don't leave me. I would be so lost without you."

Afraid that Claire may give in to her emotions and be unable to hold them together, I joined her on her side of the bed and whispered. "He will wake up soon, I am sure of it. Be strong, okay. Remember, he might be able to hear you. I know he loves you so much, Claire. He won't leave you."

Claire turned and collapsed into my arms. "I'm trying so hard not to fall apart, but it's so damn hard. I just want him to wake up and smile at me. I want things to be how they were this morning when he made love to me and held me in his arms before getting up to make me coffee."

"And he will again." I paused before speaking again. "Claire, do you want me to stay with you tonight?"

Claire pulled herself away and furrowed her brow. "You would do that?"

"Of course. The thought of you going home alone to an empty apartment doesn't sit well with me."

"Jill, I am touched. It wouldn't be too weird for you?"

"Claire, I told you I am here for you. I'm excited about you and Travis and your future together. We never had one, and I may be his ex-girlfriend, but it doesn't mean I can't still care about him. In fact, I care about both of you."

Claire gave me a caring smile. "Thank you, Jill. I would love it if you stayed with me tonight as long as you don't mind the couch."

"It's fine. I just need to swing by my house and grab a few things. I'll call my roommate Sadie and let her know. She'll probably be at her boyfriend's house, anyway. I never see her anymore."

"I'm sorry. I got the impression you were close friends."

"We were together for a while when Travis and I broke up. I think I needed someone to lean on, and she was there. But I see we are drifting apart. I'm expecting her to tell me she is moving in with Logan any day now. She hasn't been home in days."

"What will you do if she does?"

I waved my hands. "I'm not going to think about that right now. I'll deal with it when and if it happens. But right now, I want to be here for you and Travis. That's what is important."

Claire and I bonded even more while we sat close to Travis, and I wondered if Travis was listening in on our conversations. I felt comfortable sharing with her how Travis and I first met at a bar, and I never made it home. It was the first time I had gone home with someone within hours of first meeting them. Claire shared with me how her relationship with Travis developed over time, but the attraction was strong from the beginning. Funny, yesterday morning, I would never have dreamt of having such a conversation with her.

I felt no jealousy towards her whatsoever, and it felt good. I felt confident about our newfound friendship and believed we had a future as close friends.

"Claire, we've been here for over an hour. Do you think we should let the others come in for a while?" I mentioned to her as she continued to stare down at Travis.

Claire looked down at Travis. "Just give me a little longer. I can't bear the thought of leaving him. What if he wakes up?"

"You don't live that far from here, right? You need to get some rest. You will be no good tomorrow if you don't. If there are any changes, the hospital will call you."

"You're right, and I want to go talk to the doctors and nurses. I plan on being here by his side all day tomorrow."

"I understand, and I'm sure work will too."

"I have two weeks' paid vacation due. I'm going to use it."

"Good idea." I took her hand. Come on. I'll leave you to talk to the doctor while I head back to the waiting area and tell the others they can see Travis now. I'll meet you there, okay?"

"Sounds good." Claire agreed and let go of my hand. She leaned into Travis and kissed him tenderly on the cheek. Her lips trembled as she spoke. "I'll be back soon, my love. I will miss you in our bed tonight. I love you, Travis. I hope you can hear me."

When I returned to the lobby, I found only Ricky sitting in one of the chairs. He immediately stood and approached me. Not wanting to lose myself in the seduction of his stare, I stood nervously, unsure how to act, and lowered my eyes. His warm breath tingled my skin when he spoke.

"Hey. How is he doing?"

"He looks peaceful. I just hope he isn't in any pain. His face is pretty messed up, but the rest of him looks okay except for the damn coma." I tilted back my head. God, I hope he wakes up soon. My biggest fear is that he could be in that state for months, if not years, but I won't tell Claire that. I've heard stories of people being in a coma for years."

Ricky caught me by surprise when he took my hand and gave it a gentle squeeze. His skin was warm, and I welcomed his touch. I tried to erase the sinful thoughts that were circling in my head. This was not the time or place.

"We have to believe that he will pull through and make a full recovery. We can never give up. One day soon, Travis will be here with us again." He told me with eyes locked on mine.

His eyes stole my heart when I raised my head and gave him a weak smile. "I hope you are right." I needed to focus on the conversation and not listen to my pounding heart. After scanning the area where we stood, I found the courage to speak again. "Where did Slater and Sabela go?"

"To the cafeteria."

Ricky gave me a warm smile and squeezed my hand again. "Which gives me some time to get to know you better."

# CHAPTER 8

*I* was certain my cheeks had turned a shade of red and pulled away from Ricky's hand. "I need to sit down."

His voice was soothing but yet sexy. "Are you okay?"

After shaking my head to brush off the repetitive, sinful thoughts, I was having. I told myself I was not attracted to this man, and if I was, I needed to stop it. Travis is fighting for his life. Now is not the place or time to start something with someone.

Ricky supported my elbow as I eased myself down into a nearby chair and took a deep breath.

"Can I get you some water?" he asked me.

"Yeah, that would be good, thanks."

He stepped over to the nearby table and grabbed one of the three bottles. "Here you go. They've been sitting there for a while. It's not cold. Is that okay?"

I nodded and held out my hand. "Yeah, that's fine. My mouth is so dry." After taking a large sip, I smacked my lips. "Thanks."

Ricky took a seat next to me. "How long have you known Slater?"

My heart pounded again, and I tried to ignore it. "I've known

Sabela longer. At least four years. We used to work together at the dental office where I work. When she met Slater, she ran into some trouble at work and began working with him in construction. They seem happy together. They make a good couple."

"Yeah, they are amazing people. I hope to have what they have someday. How about you? Are you dating or married?"

"No. Travis and I recently broke up. I'm taking a break from the dating scene."

"I like how you are still friends. It shows how mature you are."

I wasn't about to admit that I had a life-changing event when I saw Travis limp in the cab of his truck. I still felt ashamed that it took the accident to make me realize how horrible I had been to him. I quickly reversed the conversation onto him. "What about you? Are you dating or married?"

"Nah. I'm single too. Still waiting for that special someone."

"I'm sure you will find her someday."

He threw me a wink and smiled. "Oh, I know I will. She might even be closer than I think."

Thankful that Sabela and Slater returned and I wouldn't have to reply to his last remark, I quickly stood to greet them.

"Hey, I'm waiting for Claire. She is talking to the doctors, and then I'm going to spend the night at her place. She doesn't want to be alone." I told them.

"That's nice of you, Jill," Sabela said before setting her coffee on the table next to the water.

"You can see Travis now. He is in the ICU, room 208. Let us know if there are any changes. I don't care what time it is, and I'm sure Claire would say the same."

"Of course. Get some rest. There's nothing either of you can do here."

"Claire is taking two weeks off from work. She will be here early in the morning. God, I wish I had some vacation pay. I don't know how I am going to stay focused at work tomorrow."

Slater approached me. "Look, Jill. If you need a few days off, I can help you out. You don't have to pay me back either. I want to help you."

Tears pooled in my eyes. "Oh, Slater, that is the sweetest thing. I don't know what to say?"

Sabela took my hand. "Let him help you, Jill. You can't go to work. I'm sure Dr. Larson will understand."

"Did you guys win the lottery or something?" I asked Slater with a furrowed brow.

"Oh, I guess you hadn't heard," Sabela said and glanced over at Slater, who gave her a slight nod, which I assumed meant it was okay to tell me. "Eve, the mother of his son, passed away and left everything to Slater. She was quite wealthy. So you see, he can help you."

"Oh wow! I have been in the dark for too long. Fill me in some time. I appreciate the offer, and I will seriously think about it." I smiled. "Thank you."

Slater pulled his hand out of his front pocket and walked over to me. "It's the least I can do. I've known you as long as I've known Travis. He is like a brother to me. You guys may not be together anymore, but I consider you both family. I know Travis would approve of it too."

"Thank you, Slater. That means a lot. I'll let you know." I looked over his shoulder. "Here comes Claire."

We all stood in silence, and when Claire neared us, Slater spoke first. "What did the doctor tell you?"

"The same thing you guys said. Go home and get some rest. They will call me if there are any changes. He told me it's a waiting game. His vital signs are holding steady, and his face should heal nicely. They hope that when the swelling on his brain subsides, he will wake up. They do not know if he will have any permanent side effects from the coma until he is conscious." Tears pooled in her eyes again. "I'm so scared. What if he does?"

Slater was the closest to her and took her in his arm. "Shh. Travis is a strong dude. I'm certain he is going to make a full recovery. Now, why don't you go home? Take a hot bath and get a good night's sleep. You need to rest for Travis."

Claire wiped a tear that had escaped. "Thank you all for being here. I'll call you in the morning."

Ricky took me by surprise as I stood and picked up my pink purse from the floor. "Let me walk you ladies out to your car. I don't like the idea of you walking through a dimly lit parking lot at night."

"Thank you, Ricky," Claire replied. "We would like that, wouldn't we, Jill?"

"Er, sure." Thanks, Ricky.

He directed his smile at me when he spoke. "It would be my pleasure." He said, followed by a wink.

After we said our goodbyes to Slater and Sabela, Ricky walked between Claire and me and led us to my car. Claire immediately stepped in when I unlocked the door with the button on my keys and thanked Ricky when she was seated.

He reached my side before me and surprised me when he opened the door. He scanned the car. "Pink, eh?"

"Yep. My favorite color."

I lowered my eyes from his stare. "Thanks for getting the door," stepping into the car. My hands felt clammy as I searched for the ignition and quickly started the motor when I finally found them. With the engine in idle, Ricky closed my door and lowered his head to the level of my eyes. "I hope I see you again soon. Will you be here tomorrow?"

"I'm not sure. I need to talk to my boss. Claire won't be going in, and if I don't, he will be short-handed."

"Maybe after work?" he asked.

"Yes, most definitely."

He grinned. "Then I will be here too."

# CHAPTER 9

*R*icky stood off to the side and smiled as I pulled out of my space. A part of me wanted to stay and get to know him better, but I just couldn't under the circumstances. It would feel too weird and not to mention wrong. I was flirting with a guy when I was supposed to give Claire support while Travis is fighting for his life.

"How are you doing, Claire?" I asked while watching Ricky fade in my rearview mirror.

"I'm doing okay. Thank you for coming home with me tonight."

"You don't have to thank me. I wouldn't have it any other way. I don't need to go to my place. I can make do with what I have and go home tomorrow to change and freshen up after I drop you off at the hospital. Now how do we get to your place?"

Claire played navigator as I drove, and within fifteen minutes, we were parked outside her condo, which I suddenly realized was now also Travis's home. I waited while Claire rummaged through her purse for her keys. "Here they are." She said, holding them up. "Poor Tilly has not been out all day. I'm normally home hours ago."

"Well, she will be happy to see you," I joked.

Before we even approached her door, the sound of Tilly's barks could be heard and echoed down the narrow hallway.

"Okay, Tilly. I'm coming." Claire called and quickened her pace.

I waited patiently a few steps back as Claire fumbled with her keys and opened the front door. Tilly immediately appeared and ran in circles around Claire's feet.

Claire knelt on one knee. "Hey, baby girl. Mommy is so sorry." She laughed when Tilly jumped up into her arms. "Come on in and make yourself at home. I'm going to take her outside really quickly."

I nodded and entered the condo while Claire reached for a red leash and snapped it onto Tilly's collar. "She is adorable," I said, bending down to give her a friendly pet.

"Yeah, she's my baby girl—spoiled rotten. I'll be back in a jiffy. There is beer in the fridge if you want one. I know I will when I get back."

"Thanks. I think I will."

After Claire had left, I glanced around the room, and it felt strange seeing what I recognized to be Travis's things. A pair of his shoes sat by the front door, a denim shirt draped over the back of the couch, and a few of his motorcycle books on the coffee table. A photo on the bookshelves caught my eye, and I walked across the room to inspect it. It was a picture of Claire and Travis in a kiss. Her arms were draped around his neck, and his were cradled around her waist. Claire stood on one leg with her other foot pointed back. They looked happy and in love. I wondered where they were and who had taken the picture. They were in someone's home, but I didn't know who's.

I smiled at the large picture of Tilly on the wall as I turned and resumed my hunt for a beer. Claire returned ten minutes later with a happy and excited Tilly that had just released a day's worth of pee. I laughed when she jumped into my lap on the couch where I sat and smothered my face with puppy breath and wet kisses.

"Tilly, get down. I'm so sorry. She has no manners."

"She's fine. I've been thinking about getting a cat, but I may change my mind and get myself a friendly little dog like this. She is adorable."

Claire stood before me and picked Tilly off my lap. "Come on, girl. I still need to feed you." She said as she carried her into the kitchen.

"Did you find a beer?" Claire called from the other room.

"Yes, Thanks, I did."

A few minutes later, she returned with a beer in hand and took a seat next to me on the couch. "Are you sure this couch will be big enough for you?"

"Sure. It will be fine. You have a beautiful place." I closed my eyes for a second and corrected myself. "I'm sorry. You and Travis have a beautiful home."

Claire gave me a caring smile. "Thanks. Are you sure you are going to be okay here? It's not too weird for you?"

I shook my head. "No, it's fine. I told you. I am perfectly fine. In fact, while you were outside, I was admiring the picture of you and Travis on the bookshelf. You both look so happy. Where was it taken?"

Claire glanced in the direction where the picture sat. "At Slater and Sabela's place. It was our first time there, and Travis proposed to me that night. Sabela took the picture."

"I am happy for the two of you."

Claire smiled again. "Thank you." She leaned back and took a swig of her beer. "I'm going to finish this and call it a night. I'm so drained. I hope I can sleep. I can't get Travis out of my mind. Seeing him lying there in that hospital bed. Helpless and not knowing I was there holding his hand and kissing him tore at my heart."

"I know, and I feel terrible that it took something like this to be nice to you finally. I've been such a bitch. Why didn't you slap me or something?"

Claire laughed. It was good to see her smile. "Trust me; I have wanted to many times." She took another swig of beer. "Did you know Travis never knew his birth parents?"

I nodded. "I did. He told me once, but the old me back then was so wrapped up in herself that I didn't pay any attention. He mentioned it once when he showed me some photos of him as a kid, and that was it, end of the conversation."

"I've been thinking a lot about it today since seeing Travis in the hospital. Somewhere out there are his parents, and they have no idea that a child they had is fighting for his life. And I hate to even think this because it terrifies me. But what if Travis doesn't make it? They will never have the chance to meet their son. That is so sad. I can't help thinking about it."

"What are you saying?"

"I have no idea where to start, but I think I want to look for his parents."

I whispered. "Do you think Travis would approve?"

Claire nodded. "I do. We had an intense conversation after he had told me, and I had bought it up. Put it this way he didn't say no."

"Wow. You guys talk about everything, don't you?"

Claire chuckled. "Well, how else am I going to get to know him?" She leaned her head back into the pillow of the couch and looked up to the ceiling. "Question is, where does one begin to look for lost parents?"

"You could try social media and that site Ancestory.com. Maybe post some of those pictures of when he was a kid."

Claire sat up. "I haven't seen them. Would they be here?"

I glanced around the room. "They should be. He didn't leave them at my house. He always kept them in a shoebox."

Claire took my hand and pulled me up to my feet. "Come with me. He has some boxes in the closet."

"Okay," I said, uncertain how Travis would react to me, his ex, going through his things.

When we walked through the bedroom, images flashed

through my head of Travis and Claire making love in the large king-size bed before me. I came to a sudden stop and was about to leave the room when Claire turned and saw me standing in the room, staring away from the bed.

"Are you okay?"

I couldn't tell her. "Yeah, I'm fine. I just got dizzy, that's all."

"Do you want to sit down on the bed?"

I quickly shook my head and put one foot in front of the other. "No. No. I'm good. It's probably from all the trauma today. I'll be fine. Come on, show me those boxes." I followed Claire into the closet and immediately recognized all of Travis's clothes hanging on the left. Claire's hung on the right. She pointed to the top shelf above his clothes.

"You are taller than me. Can you reach those? There are three of them."

Stretching my body to the max, I slid the boxes to the edge of the shelf and gave them a slight nudge until they pivoted and fell into my arms. "Got them."

"Great. Let's take them to the living room."

"I followed and with care slid them from my arms onto the coffee table."

"Do you want another beer?" Claire asked.

"I thought you were going to bed?"

She shook her hands. "Not now. I want to see if those pictures are in one of those boxes."

After bringing out two more beers, Claire joined me on the couch. We both took some beer before Claire reached for a box, slowly peeling off the lid, and sat it on the table.

I leaned in closer to inspect the contents. "Doesn't look like photos to me," I said.

Claire picked up a few of the items. "These are all receipts. Must be his taxes or something."

"Probably. He would always keep receipts for a few years after filing." I handed her the lid. "What's in the next one?"

Claire pulled it onto her lap and removed the lid. "More receipts."

"Okay, one more box to go," I said as I handed it to her while taking the other from her.

Claire took a deep breath and slowly pulled back the lid. She released a heavy sigh of disappointment. "More damn receipts."

"He must have one box for each year of taxes." I glanced around the room. "Where else would he have boxes?"

Claire was silent. Deep in thought. "Let me think." Suddenly, her eyes lit up. "I know!" Maybe the dresser. I gave him the left side. She quickly rose to her feet. "Come on, let's go check. It's in the bedroom."

Tilly heard the command come on and left the comfort of her bed to follow us into the bedroom. Claire wasted no time and began pulling out the drawers on the left side. She struggled with the bottom one. It was stuck, and it took the two of us to pull it open far enough so we could see the contents inside.

"I see a shoebox in the back," Claire said as she grabbed it and pulled it free out of the drawer. She didn't bother to take it back to the living room. Instead, she sat on the edge of the bed and pried off the lid and then gasped before looking my way with wide eyes. "It's photos. I think this is it." Claire pulled out a handful of loose pictures.

I took a seat next to her, trying hard not to think I was sitting on the bed where she makes love to Travis. "I think you are right," I replied as I reached in and grabbed some pictures.

Claire held up a picture so I could see it. "Look, this is a birthday party, and I bet you that is Travis blowing out the candles." She looked up and pointed to the lady standing next to him, smiling. "And who is that woman? I wonder if she is one of the foster parents. She may know about Travis's history."

"This is the box. I remember some of these photos. He was about eight in that picture."

Claire studied the picture some more. "I wonder where all

these kids are. They must be the same age as Travis now—almost thirty."

Claire's voice raised a notch from her excitement. "Jill. This is just one picture. There are dozens in here. I need to look through these and see how I can use them to help locate his parents."

"Well, like I said, you could post some on social media. See if anyone recognizes them."

Claire's eyes were wide as she picked up another photo. "Look at this one. It's a little boy, younger than the birthday one."

I took the picture and studied it. "It's the same boy, though. It must be Travis. The woman is not the same."

"If that's Travis. I'm guessing he was about four. They must be some other foster parents. He said he had a lot. No one could handle him."

I'm going to go through these and do what you suggested. Post them online. Will you help me?"

"Tonight? I thought you were tired. You want to be at the hospital early. Remember."

Claire waved her hand in the air. "How can I go to sleep with these?" Claire sat on the other side of the bed and emptied the photos into the quilt. "Come on. Help me find some with grown-ups. Those are the ones that may know something about his past." Claire said while spreading the photos on the bed.

I rolled my eyes. She may have a second burst of energy stemming from finding the photos. But I could feel myself fading. "Okay, but just for a little while. We both need to get some sleep."

Claire wasn't listening. "Here is another one. It's a man with whom I am guessing is Travis. It's the same guy as the one with the woman. Travis looks to be the same age. Around four, and Travis is holding a football." She looked at the picture closer. "It's the same house. I wonder where it is."

While Claire was reeling off her investigation work, another picture caught my eye. "Look at this one. It's outside a school. It says Clifford elementary. It looks like a class photo. One of them must be Travis."

Claire quickly pulled it from my hands. "Let me see. Wow. Where is Clifford Elementary?" She pointed at a specific boy. "This looks like him. Have you heard of this school?"

I laughed. Why would I know of this school? I don't have any kids. Look on the internet. Everything is on there."

"Good idea. Where is my phone?" Claire pulled herself off the bed. "I'll be right back."

I nodded while browsing through more of the pictures.

A few minutes later, Claire returned and resumed her place on the bed. I watched as she began tapping on her phone. "Shoot, there are six Clifford schools in six different states."

"Did Travis ever say he lived in other states?"

"No, he didn't, and here is one in California. It's in Manteca." She looked up and creased her brow. "Where's that?"

"Isn't there a map?"

"Oh, yeah." Claire clicked and then zoomed out the map. "It's up north near Modesto."

"Oh, okay. I've heard of that. It's somewhere up near San Francisco. So what do you want to do? Post these pictures and then what?"

"I don't know. Maybe call the school and go from there. It's a start, don't you think?"

"It sure is."

"Let's do it now."

"What? You mean call the school? There's no one there at this hour. Like any smart human being, they are probably asleep. Unlike us." I joked.

"No, silly. The photos. Let's post the pictures now. We might wake up to some responses."

I chuckled. "You already made up your mind, didn't you? You are not going to bed until you've posted these, are you?"

"That's right. It will only take a minute. Let's take the pictures out to the living room and use my laptop." Claire said as she gathered up the photos and put them in the shoebox.

Claire was right. Within fifteen minutes, we had posted six photos onto Facebook. I listened as she read the text we had written together out loud. "Need your help. Does anyone recognize anyone in these pictures dating from twenty to twenty-five years ago? Any information would be helpful. Please tag anyone that you think might. I'm desperately trying to find my fiancée's birth parents. They were only fifteen when they had him. His name is Travis Kent. Feel free to private message me. Thank you." Claire released a satisfactory smile. "I like that. Okay, now we can go to bed."

"Yeah. I'm getting tired now." Claire said through a yawn.

"Finally." When I stood, I stretched and released a loud yawn. I smiled when I saw Tilly curled up on one of the pillows on the bed. "Are you going to leave her there?"

"Yeah, that's Travis's pillow. She probably misses him."

I pictured Travis sleeping where Tilly rested, and I quickly shook my head. "Okay, I'm off to get some sleep. I'll see you in the morning."

"I hope I can sleep. I'm going to be tossing all night wondering if anyone has answered our post. What if someone does?"

# CHAPTER 10

W ater running and the clinking of dishes woke me from what little sleep I had savored on the two-person couch. Claire was right. It was too small. My knees had been bent all night, and I struggled to straighten them when I tried to pull my cramped body off the cushions. "Claire, is that you?" I called as I stood to my feet.

Claire appeared in the doorway, fully dressed. "Sorry, did I wake you?"

"No, I was already awake." I lied. "What time is it?"

"A little before six. I want to be at the hospital by seven if that's okay. I'll call work from there."

"Yeah, that's fine. Do you have any coffee?"

"Yes, I do. I'm making some right now. I'll get the pot going, and then I'll take Tilly out while it's brewing. Help yourself."

"Thanks."

"I checked the post as soon as I woke up, and no one has responded. That's pretty disappointing." Claire said with a frown.

I released a slight chuckle. "Claire, it's only been a few hours. Give it some time."

"I know I'm just anxious." She grabbed Tilly's leash from behind the door, and instantly Tilly appeared at her feet. "I'll be back. I'm going to take Tilly out."

By 6:45, Claire and I were in my car, driving to the hospital. One thing I noticed was how punctual Claire was. It shouldn't come as no surprise, though. I can't ever remember a day when she was late for work. As much as I wanted to stay at the hospital with her, I desperately needed to get home and freshen up and get the sour taste out lingering in my mouth from not brushing my teeth. And a shower and fresh clothes would not be a bad idea either.

"Are you going to call Dr. Larson when you get to the hospital?"

Claire nodded. "Yeah, he doesn't get in until around 8:30. Have you decided if you are going to take some time off too? Slater said he would help you."

"I don't know. It would feel weird taking money from him. And besides, how would Dr. Larson manage with the two of us not there? I'll think about it on my way home."

Claire nodded. "Well, I think you should." She replied as I put the car in park. "Are you coming in?"

"Yes, of course. I want to see how Travis is doing."

The nurse allowed us to go to Travis's room straight away and told us doctor Ryan would be on duty in about an hour.

Travis looked exactly how we had left him. Soft music played from the wall speakers, and the shades were drawn.

Claire pulled a chair from against the wall and placed it by the side of his bed. "He hasn't moved at all," she whispered, taking his hand. "Hi, Travis. I'm back. It was so lonely at home without you. Tilly slept on your pillow last night. She misses you too."

I remained silent and let Claire have her time with Travis. I wondered if he could hear her.

"Jill is with me, too. She spent the night at our place. I didn't want to go home alone, and Jill offered to stay." Claire turned her head at me and smiled. "It's amazing after how we started. We are friends now. You brought us together, Travis. We both care about you so much, and we want you back." Claire stood, leaned in, and kissed Travis's cheek. "I love you, Travis. I want you to come home."

I strolled across the room and placed my hand on Claire's shoulder while I looked down at Travis. He looked so peaceful. His face was still swollen, and the skin around his swollen eyes was now a deep purple and black. "She's right, Travis. We both care about you. We can't wait to see you open your eyes. We will be here waiting for that day."

Claire took my hand and squeezed it. "God, I hope he wakes up soon."

"Me too. I will leave you two alone and let you talk to the doctor while I run home and change out of these clothes. I'll be back in an hour. Will you be okay?"

"Yeah. This is where I want to be."

I returned home to an empty house. It looked like Sadie had not been home. Everything was how I had left it yesterday morning. I checked my messages and saw there were three from Sadie. I had been so wrapped up with the events of yesterday that I hadn't checked my messages all day.

*Jill Doctor Larson told me about Travis's accident. My god, is he okay? Call me.*

*Jill, I've not heard from you. Please call me.*

*Jill, will you please call me? Are you okay? Is Travis okay?*

After texting Sadie back and filling her in on Travis's condition, I wasted no time jumping in the shower and putting on fresh clothes. By the time I felt human again, it was almost eight-fifteen, and I still hadn't decided whether I was going to work. My phone dinged, and I glanced at the screen. It was Sadie.

*I'm so sorry. I'm just heading to work. We will talk more when you get there.*

I knew then I couldn't go to work. I wasn't ready to replay the accident that kept playing in my head aloud to Dr. Larson and

Sadie and answer all their questions. I would just break down. They would just have to manage without me. He can call a temp service. Anyone can answer phones and write dates on a computer. I can afford to take a few days off, but I won't take any money from Slater.

When 8:30 rolled around, I called work. Sadie answered the phone.

"Hi Sadie, it's Jill. I need to talk to Dr. Larson."

"Jill! Are you okay? My god, I've been so worried about you. I'm sorry I've not been home. Are you on your way?"

I hated that I had to go through Sadie to reach my boss. "I'm okay. Thanks. I'm not coming in today. I didn't get much sleep. Can you put me through to Dr. Larson?"

"Can I do anything for you?"

"No. I just need to talk to Dr. Larson. Can you put me through?" I asked again.

"Are you sure there is nothing I can do? I feel terrible that I've been gone."

Sadie continued to ignore my requests, and my patience was fading fast. "Sadie, I have to get back to the hospital. Will you please just put me through?"

"Is he still in a coma?"

I raised my voice. "Yes, he is still in a coma. I need to talk to Dr. Larson and let him know I'm not coming in."

"Sorry, one second."

I released a heavy sigh of relief. "Thank you. I'll call you when I can."

A few minutes later, Dr. Larson came on the line, and after telling him my request, he granted it with no hesitation and told me to take as much time as I needed, and he even said if I needed it, he would advance me two weeks, vacation pay. Wow! I thanked him and told him I would keep in touch.

On my drive back to the hospital, I weighed the idea in my

head of Dr. Larson's offer. Claire needed someone right now, and I could help her with her quest of finding Travis's birth parents. I could also be with her at the hospital much more, and I could take Tilly for walks. I also needed time to process everything that has happened and somehow stop the movie of the accident from playing repeatedly in my head.

# CHAPTER 11

Claire hadn't left Travis's side since I had left. She sat next to him, talking to him while holding his hand. She turned and gave me a weak smile when I entered the room.

"Hi," she whispered.

"Hey," I whispered back. "Did you talk to the doctor?"

"I did. He said all his vitals are good. All we can do is wait. I hate this so much." Tears pooled in her eyes.

"I know you do, Claire. I hate it too. But I've decided I'm going to be here for you in any way I can. I called work and told Dr. Larson I needed some time off. He agreed and told me to take off as much time as I wanted." I smiled. "He's even going to advance my vacation pay. I have already used up what I had for this year. I can't see you going through this alone. I can stay at your condo if you want for as long as you need me. I'd be happy to help with Tilly."

"Thank you so much, Jill. I would love that. You are a good person. My mom and dad called too, and they offered to help as well. They are going to come by later."

I chuckled. I never remembered anyone calling me a good person. "Now it seems I am. I'm liking the new me."

"I definitely am." Claire laughed. "Travis is going to be so surprised when he wakes up and finds out we are now friends. So much has happened."

"I know."

"I'm not going to leave his side. I want to be here all day. What if he wakes up when I am gone?" Claire confessed.

"I don't blame you. I will be here with you. I can get you some breakfast or coffee if you want."

"No. I'm not hungry. Thanks. I was thinking, though. Would it be too much trouble for you to go by my place and grab my laptop? I can't read on these damn phones. I want to research looking for Travis's parents some more. We could do it together."

"Sure, not a problem. I'll take Tilly for a walk too."

Claire looked at me and creased her brow. "I don't think I've ever seen you without any makeup. I like it. You look fresh."

"I think it's a first for me. I just wasn't in the mood this morning. Funny, last week, I wouldn't have cared if putting on my face was going to make me late. I would never leave my home without it." I glanced at Travis. "It's all your fault, Travis." I joked. "Okay, I will be back in a bit. Need anything else?"

"No, I'm okay. I'll see you soon."

When I returned an hour later with Claire's laptop wedged under my arm, I realized I hadn't eaten all day, and it was now almost one o'clock. I wondered if Claire had. She was not sitting on the chair where I expected to find her. I turned my head in the dimly lit room and found her standing at the end of the bed, humming a tune while she massaged Travis's feet.

I closed the door behind me. "What are you doing?"

"Rubbing his feet." Dr. Ryan suggested it. It keeps the blood flowing and may stimulate a reaction from him. If I feel even a toe twitch, he wants me to tell him or the nurses."

"Anything yet?"

Claire shook her head. "No, but I'll keep doing this every fifteen minutes or so."

"Have you eaten?"

"No. I can't. I'm just too afraid to leave him."

"You have to eat something, Claire. You have to stay strong for Travis. What good will you be to him if you fall sick?"

Claire knew I was right and nodded. "Can you bring me something from the Cafeteria?"

"Of course. How about a sandwich and some milk?"

"Yeah. That will be good, thanks."

"Oh, here is your laptop. I'll leave it here on this desk."

"Great, we can research together. I can't believe the only comments I am getting on my Facebook post are a bunch of good luck."

Over a couple of stale sandwiches and many cups of coffee, Claire and I browsed the internet for ideas on ways to find Travis's birth parents.

"Was he ever adopted?" I asked.

"No, he was a troubled kid and was shuffled from foster home to foster home. I know he spent some time in the juvenile hall, but I have no idea where. I know his birth name is Kent, which, if I understand correctly, if the parents are not married or if the father is not in the picture, the child is given the birth mother's name?"

"Yeah, I've heard that before, too. Surely he has some kind of birth certificate?"

Claire shrugged her shoulders. I have no idea. We didn't get that far in the conversation. But he must have something, and the mother's name should be listed on it. Why did he tell me he didn't know her name?"

"Well, maybe he has never seen it?"

Claire shook her head. "No, I don't believe that. You need a birth certificate for a driver's license."

While Claire gave Travis's feet another rubbing session, I emailed the elementary school from the photo we had found and a copy of the picture I had taken with my phone, asking for any information. I also emailed a dozen agencies and foster agencies, asking them for any advice. "Okay, I'm done. Now cross your fingers, we get some replies. I can't think of anything else we can do."

"Me neither." Claire smiled. "I really appreciate you, Jill. Thank you." She picked up her phone lying on the bed and glanced at it. "It's almost five. Slater and Sabela said they would come by around six. My parents text me, and they are on their way."

"Okay. Well, that gives me enough time to run back to your place, feed, and take Tilly out. That way, you can spend some time with your mom and dad."

"Thank you so much. I don't know what I would do without you."

After hugging Claire, I grabbed my purse and left the room only to see Ricky at the other end of the hallway walking towards me.

# CHAPTER 12

*I* froze with my hand still on the door handle and contemplated going back into the room, but I decided that was just foolish and told myself to stop being stupid. My hand felt clammy as it clung to the cold metal of the handle, and I quickly released it and folded my arms in front of me as I walked in his direction. Butterflies churned in my stomach, and my heart pounded beneath my chest. I didn't know where to look. I was a bundle of nervous energy and felt like a kid out of high school.

When we were a few feet apart, he winked and smiled and raked his hand through his peppered blonde hair. He hadn't shaved, which was even more appealing to me, and he wore faded jeans and a black t-shirt. "Hey, Jill. I didn't think I'd see you till tonight."

I gave him a nervous laugh. Unsure what to do with my hands, I slid them into the back pockets of my jeans. "Oh, I've been helping Claire. She's been here all day. I didn't know you were coming by."

"Yeah. Slater is coming by soon, and I need to grab some tools out of his truck. He asked if I could help him until Travis gets better."

"Ahh, I see."

There was a moment of uncomfortable silence. I had no idea what to say next and waited, feeling awkward.

"Say. Are you coming back later? Do you want to grab a bite to eat?"

Part of me wanted to say yes, but I couldn't help but feel uncomfortable about the whole thing. "I'm sorry, but I don't think that would be such a good idea considering the circumstances with Travis and everything."

Ricky creased his brow. "I wasn't asking you out on a date—just a friendly meal between two people. That's all. A chance to get to know you. I know everyone else here but you."

He sounded agitated. I can't say I blame him. "I'm sorry. Maybe some other time. I wouldn't be in very good company right now."

His eyes lit up just a tad, as if he understood, and he nodded. "I'm sorry. How insensitive of me. Of course, I understand." He winked again. "Well, I'm glad you are not blowing me off completely. That would hurt my feelings."

I liked his sense of humor, and he stirred something inside of me. "No, I'm not blowing you off. I'm just not up to socializing right now. I think I will be better in a few days. I'm just so worried about Travis."

Ricky reached out and rested his hand on my shoulder. "It's okay. You don't have to explain. I think we are all in shock right now. I'm just trying to be a friend. That's all. Nothing more."

His touch took me by surprise, but at the same time, I welcomed it, and then I lost it. I collapsed into his arms and let the tears pour. The emotions I had been holding back to be strong for Claire suddenly burst. "Oh, thank you. I'm such a mess. What if Travis never recovers?"

Ricky caught me in his arms, and I rested my head on his firm chest and welcomed his strong embrace. "Hey. Everything is going to be okay. You have to believe that. I do. If I didn't, I'd be a mess like you." He chuckled.

I had to snicker through my tears at his joke. He was right. I had to pull myself out of this rut. "I know, but it's tough. I feel guilty for living when Travis is in that room fighting for his life. It's just not fair. The thought of having a good time or doing anything fun just seems so wrong. Even having a friendly lunch or dinner with you."

Ricky held my upper arms with his hands and gave me a little shake before looking into my eyes. "It's okay to feel the way you do, but you have to ask yourself. Would Travis like it?"

I wiped my moist cheeks and sniffed back the last of my tears. "Travis and I were not friends before the accident. We had a bad breakup, which was all my fault. I was a bitch to him and Claire. I want to apologize to him, and I'm afraid I won't have the chance to."

Ricky continued to humor me. "You were a bitch? Nah, not you. I can't see that."

Whatever he was doing was working. I chuckled. "Oh, I was a total bitch. You would not have wanted anything to do with me a week or two ago. Didn't Travis ever talk to you about his ex- Jill? Well, that's me." I said, followed by a sarcastic smile.

"For your information, no, he never did. I knew he was going through a breakup. He had mentioned it once when he was short-tempered at work. But he never bad-mouthed you."

I had to admit I was surprised by what Ricky had told me after the way I had treated Travis. During the last year I was with him, I never saw the good in him I had seen when we first met. When we fought, it was because I knew how to push his buttons and set him off. Travis never started the fights; it was always me. "Well, I thank Travis for that," I told Ricky, stunned, because he had plenty of ammo to tarnish my name.

"So, where are you off to?" Rickey asked.

"I'm on my way to go to Claire's condo and take care of her dog."

Ricky paused for a moment, releasing a subtle smile. "Would you like some company?"

I hesitated. "Er, sure. But remember, I won't be very good company."

"That's okay. I'll make up for it," he joked.

"Wait, what about the tools you are supposed to get from Slater?"

"Oh, I can get those when we get back. He will still be here." He pulled out his phone from his back pocket. "I'll text him."

I gave him a friendly smile. "Okay then, sure, I would love some company. Thank you."

"Great. Are you parked out front?" he chuckled, raising his brow. Wait, are you driving that pink Mustang?"

"Yes, why? You don't like my car?"

"It's not that I don't like it. It's just not my color."

I laughed. "You don't like pink. Shame on you."

"How about I give you a ride in my truck?" He raised his hands. "No offense, but I'm not sure I'd be comfortable riding in a pink car. It messes with my macho image."

I laughed again. Ricky sure had a way with words that made me feel better and helped pull me out of the slump I insisted on being in. "Well, I don't want to ruin your macho ego. Sure we can ride In your truck. Just let me check with Claire that it's okay I take you to her place."

"Not a problem. I've been there before with Travis to pick up some stuff. I'm sure it will be okay. I'll go back in the room with you."

"Great, you can see Travis before we leave."

# CHAPTER 13

$C$laire couldn't hide her surprise when I checked with her and asked if she minded Ricky tagged along with me.

"Er, no, that's fine."

"It would be nice to have some company. We'll be back soon."

Claire closed her dropped jaw and nodded.

Ricky's shiny navy blue truck with a chrome running board and lights across the top of the cab was parked close to the entrance. "Nice truck," I said, climbing into the passenger side.

"Thanks. I just bought it a month ago. Slater gave me a nice raise."

"That was nice of him. I hear he is doing really well. His ex left him some money, right?"

"Yeah, quite a bit, too. And it's also a big house. Travis told me that Slater is going to turn it into a children's foster home and that he and Claire will run it." His smile vanished. "That is if Travis is able to."

I echoed his words in disbelief. "He is going to have Travis and Claire run it?"

"Yes. You didn't know?"

I felt the heat in my cheeks rise and my mood change. The news disturbed me. "No, I didn't know. No one told me. I've been with Claire for the past two days. Why the hell didn't she say something?" I thought back to our last conversation at work before the accident. Claire had mentioned to me she would give her two weeks' notice. It all made sense now. Here I was, helping her and running back and forth to bring her the laptop, feed Tilly, get her breakfast, and she couldn't even tell me about this. Anger had set in. "I can't believe she didn't tell me."

Ricky picked up on my altered mood and tried to calm me while he fired up the truck. "Well, I'm sure she was planning on telling you, but then the accident happened. Maybe it's not the right time for her."

"Yeah, I know. But still. This is huge. I was with her all last night at her place and most of today. She could have said something then, or even when she told me she was quitting work. Why only tell me half the story?"

Ricky narrowed his eyes. "Why does this bother you so much? Do you still have feelings for Travis or something?"

I quickly shook my head. "No, I don't have feelings for him. I don't know why it upsets me. It just does."

"Are you jealous of Claire?"

"What's with all the damn questions? Are we going to sit in this parking lot all afternoon while you try to analyze me?"

Ricky tilted his head and gave me a smirk that annoyed me. "Maybe."

I creased my brow and folded my arms across my chest. "And what is that supposed to mean? You said you wanted to get to know me. I didn't think that meant being drilled with stupid questions." I turned away and looked out of the window.

"I just want to know why you are so upset over Travis and Claire's amazing opportunity that Slater has given them. I thought you would be happy for them. That's how I feel. I think it's great."

My chest heaved, and I turned to face him again. "I am happy for them."

Ricky chuckled. "Well, you have a funny way of showing it."

"Look, maybe this was a bad idea. I don't need to explain myself to you or anyone else." I reached for the door handle. "I told you I wouldn't be good company. I'm just going to go to Claire's place on my own."

"What? Now you are just being ridiculous. Don't be so irrational."

My voice raised a notch when I spoke. "Don't call me ridiculous. Maybe we can try this another time, but right now, I want to be alone." I reached down and grabbed my purse from the floor of the truck, and pushed the door open.

"Oh, come on, Jill. Why are you so upset?"

In a rushed state, I didn't reply and pulled myself out of the truck and slammed the door behind me. Without looking back, I walked fast to my car while searching for the keys in my purse. When I was almost to my car, the loud screech of tires and burning rubber startled me. After turning my head, I saw it was Ricky speeding out of the parking lot.

"Well, that went well," I said under my breath as I unlocked my car and got in.

The reflections of my eyes in the rearview mirror caught my attention, and I began talking to myself. "Who does he think he is asking me all those questions? It's none of his damn business. I don't even know him, and he has the nerve to tell me I'm being ridiculous." I gave my eyes in the mirror a hard stare. "I have every right to be upset. Claire should have told me. I have a right to know. Shit, everyone else does." It then occurred to me that Slater and Sabela hadn't told me either. I spoke again to my puzzled eyes in the mirror. "Sabela used to tell me everything. So I was right, not only did Claire get my ex, but she also stole my friend." I fired up my car and, with force, put it in reverse and backed out. A loud horn caused me to slam on the brakes and look over my shoulder.

The front end of a blue SUV was within inches of my rear bumper. "God damn it," I yelled and skidded back into my spot to let the car pass.

"Watch where you are going." A male voice hollered from the car."

I screamed out of my window, "Oh fuck you!" and pulled out after he had sped past me. "Jerk!"

Traffic was heavy, and it took me a good twenty-five minutes to reach Claire's place. It was the last place I wanted to be. Then I remembered I had offered to spend the night. "God damn it." If someone had just told me about the foster home, I wouldn't be feeling this way. Everything was fine until Ricky opened his big mouth. And how the hell did Claire talk Travis into running some foster home? Well, she's got more power over him than I ever did. I couldn't even get Travis to go to the gym with me.

It suddenly struck me that I had not been to the gym in two days. I always tried to go for an hour after work most days. It always makes me feel better when I work up a sweat. Kickboxing would feel really good right about now. I made my decision. After taking care of Tilly, I would go to the gym for an hour before heading back to the hospital. I needed to work off some of this anger energy that was consuming me.

After spending a good half hour at Claire's with Tilly, I checked to see if my gym bag was on the back seat of my car and saw with relief it was.

"Hey, Jill. I've not seen you here this early before." Nancy at the front desk of the gym said, followed by her usual friendly smile.

"Yeah, I have a lot of stuff going on and took some time off work. I figured a workout would make me feel better."

"Everything okay?" Nancy asked as she tapped on her keyboard.

"Yeah, I'm okay."

"Well, you'll be happy to know this time of day is pretty quiet. Most of the machines are open."

I smiled. "Awesome. Thanks." I headed to the changing rooms, anxious to do some workouts.

Nancy wasn't kidding. I'd never seen the gym so quiet. It made sense, though; everyone was probably at work and, like me, came here at the end of the day. Some nights I would have to wait a good ten minutes or more for some of the machines.

I scanned the room. Only about half a dozen people were doing their routine workouts to beat the loud music coming from the surround sound speakers. I suddenly did a double-take and gasped. I squinted my eyes to make sure it was him. He was on a step master in front of the far mirror. His back faced me, but I could see his face in the mirror. It was definitely Ricky.

# CHAPTER 14

"What the hell is he doing here?" I snapped out loud, thankful that the music drowned my sudden shriek. "God damn it." Should I leave? I asked myself as I stood in the doorway, contemplating my options. I can't believe he is here. I've never seen him here before, and I really need this workout.

Ricky was oblivious to my presence and continued to stare at his reflection. I scanned the room for the furthest machines away from him and saw a punching bag was free in the far corner. "Perfect. I need to punch something right about now." I hissed under my breath. I snuck a quick look over at Ricky to make sure he was not looking my way and then made a dash for the isolated corner. Midway, I hear my name called out loud.

"Jill?"

I froze and squeezed my eyes shut. "Shit!"

Within seconds, Ricky was at my side. A white towel draped around his neck and beads of sweat dripped from his forehead. I might have been mad at him, but it didn't mean I couldn't notice how good he looked.

"Jill, what are you doing here?" he asked, dabbing his forehead. "Wait. Did you follow me here?" he laughed.

I tried not to pay attention to his massive, muscular arms and chest. His body was perfect in every way. Instead, I curled my lip and snarled. "No, I didn't follow you. Don't flatter yourself. I've been coming here for years." I began walking again, and when I reached for the punching bag, I dropped my towel and water and reached for the red boxing gloves hanging on the wall. After sliding them on, I gave the bag a hard punch. Damn, it felt good.

Ricky stood on the other side of the bag and gave me a hard stare while he reached for the second pair of gloves. He put them on while he spoke. "I've been coming here for years too." He gave the bag two hard hits. One from the left and then from the right. "I've never seen you here."

My eyes swallowed his stare before my first gave the bag another hard hit. "I normally come after work around five." I hit the bag again. "Maybe that's why. I never seen you here."

Ricky threw another punch, using more force. The bag swung hard in my direction; I backed away to avoid being hit by the bag.

"Yeah, I came here early when they first open. I'm usually the first one here. I like a good workout before I go to work." Ricky said with a hard stare. Suddenly, he jumped back and gave the bag a hard kick. When it swung back to him, he punched it twice. His breathing increased to a pant. "So why did you storm off? It pissed me off, you know."

The bag swung in my direction, and I mirrored Ricky's previous move with a hard kick and two punches. Sweat beaded on my brow and trickled down the middle of my back. "Well, I was pissed too." My face hid behind my gloves as I waited for the bag to return and fed it two more punches.

Ricky matched my punches on the bag. "I only told you something that I thought you already knew. I wasn't trying to start anything. Why be mad at me? Talk to Claire." He gave the bag another kick. "Or Sabela or Slater, for that matter. I have nothing to do with it."

I moved away from the bag and grabbed my towel off the floor. Sweat saturated my body. "Oh, I intend to," I replied before dabbing my face and neck. After draping the towel around my neck, I stooped over and picked up my bottle of water, and took a large swig. "It's bullshit that no one told me."

Ricky gave the bag one final punch and came and stood within inches of me. "You can hit that bag pretty hard." He smirked. "I'm impressed. It's another reason why I don't want you to be pissed off at me. I don't want to be your next punching bag."

Weakened by his presence in my space, I quickly diverted my eyes to the floor. His words softened me. "I'm not going to hit you."

Ricky lowered his head and tilted it until he looked into my eyes. "I'm not so sure about that. You have a temper. If there's no bag nearby, I better duck or run."

He had gotten to me. I released a smile, followed by a small laugh, and placed my hand on his chest, playfully pushing him away. "Oh, stop. You are making me sound terrible."

Ricky grabbed my hand and held it to his chest. His eyes pierced mine. I froze. "Jill, I like you, and I would like us to be friends. I didn't know it was going to be so difficult, though. Can we start over?" He freed my hand and stepped back. A smile appeared on his face as he held out his hand. "I'm Ricky. It's a pleasure to meet you, and you are?"

I laughed and held out my hand. "I'm Jill. It's nice to meet you too."

With a quick jerk of his hand, Rickey pulled me in, and before I had a chance to protest, his lips were on mine. My body tense, unsure how to react. It wasn't a hard, forceful kiss. It was soft, and his lips tasted like salt from the sweat surfacing on his face. My mouth remained frozen and closed, my eyes open, but the warmth from his breath was seducing me quickly.

I found the masculine scent that embraced me overpowering,

and when he let go of my hand and pulled me in by my waist, I knew I had lost the battle. I could no longer resist. My body softened; I closed my eyes and parted my lips to kiss him back. Ricky knew then he had won. In one swift move, he cupped the back of my neck with his other hand and pressed his body up against mine. His lips parted to cover mine. When I felt the softness of his tongue, I could no longer hold back and wrapped my arms around his neck to pull him in closer. The back of his neck was drenched with sweat, as well as the ends of his hair.

The level of our kiss rose a few notches; it was passionate and raw. We explored each other for the first time. I couldn't remember the last time anyone kissed me that way. I felt Ricky's hand wander, and it excited me. Unsure of where he would touch me next, I remained locked in his kiss with anticipation. Suddenly I felt the gentle strokes of his hand on the bare skin of my back, just beneath my sports bra. I gasped and pressed my lips hard against his. "Ricky. What are we doing?" I heaved while coming up for air.

Ricky panted. "I don't know." And then slid his hand down over my skin-tight pants and caressed my butt cheeks.

My head was in a tailspin. An hour ago, I wanted to punch the guy, and now I wanted him to make love to me. I pulled away and sucked in some much-needed air. My chest was pounding, and my heart raced. I raked my hand through my hair and pulled it away from my face. "My God, what the hell are you doing to me?"

Ricky approached me, His chest heaving. He ran his hand through my hair and rested it on my shoulder. "What am I doing to you? What are you doing to me? You have me all worked up. I'm not sure if I can walk." He adjusted his noticeable bulge in his gym shorts and threw me a wink.

My cheeks flushed. I laughed. "So, is this your idea of starting over?"

"Well, it's going better than the last time, don't you think?"

"Totally unexpected, I'd say." I glanced around the floor for my towel and quickly scooped it. "Look. I have to get back to the hospital. I've been gone for hours, and I still want to have that little talk with Claire."

Ricky looked surprised. "That's it. You're leaving. You are going to ignore what just happened between us? Which, by the way, I thought was pretty damn hot."

I sensed he was upset with my urge to split, but I was already feeling uncomfortable. I wasn't sure If I was ready for this. I had too much going on. I was anxious to have it out with Claire, Sabela, and Slater and, not to mention, the repeated haunting image I have of Travis lying in his hospital bed fighting for his life. To have any kind of fun just seemed so wrong right now. I'm consumed with guilt. I kept my thoughts to myself. "I'm not ignoring it. I'm just not sure if I'm ready for a relationship right now."

Ricky wiped his brow with the towel he had just draped over his neck. "You sure do a lot of thinking. Why are you trying to complicate this? I'm attracted to you. I know you are attracted to me. Normally when that happens, the two people get together. Am I missing something here?"

"I'm really sorry; I just can't do this right now. I gotta go." I turned to walk away, and Ricky grabbed my hand.

"Wait a second, Jill. Can we at least be friends? Or are you not ready for that either?"

I closed my eyes. This wasn't easy, and I liked him a lot. "Yes, I would like that."

"Okay then. So can two friends go out to dinner sometime? Say tonight?"

"Oh, Ricky, you are not making this easy. Don't get me wrong. I really like you. Do you honestly think that is such a good idea after what we just did?"

"Yes, I do. Especially after the amazing kiss we just shared. I have feelings for you, Jill, and I want to pursue them, not suppress them like you are doing."

My voice raised a notch. "No, I'm not."

"Well, what do you call it?" He shook his head. "Why are you women so hard to figure out, and why do you always say I'm not ready? What's with that?" he shook his head again. "You know what. I'm done explaining myself to you. Let me know when you are ready, if ever, and I'll let you know if I'm available. I'll see you later."

I stood and watched as Ricky stormed off and soon disappeared through the double glass doors that led to the changing rooms. Should I run after him? I wondered, fearing I just blew my only chance with him.

# CHAPTER 15

*I* didn't run after Ricky, and I'm thinking now as I drive back to the hospital that maybe I should have. I've never had to chase after a guy before, but I can't help but feel regret for telling Ricky no. I can't blame him for being mad at me. I think I panicked. The kiss happened so quickly, I wasn't expecting it. Why did he do that? Damn him. And now I've made such a mess of things, and I have no idea what to do now or how to fix it.

When I pulled into the parking lot, the first thing I saw was Ricky's truck. "Shit!" Suddenly I remembered he had to pick up some tools from Slater. "Well, this is awkward." I scanned the parking lot and found a space far away from his truck, and backed in so I could watch for when he leaves. I wasn't about to go in there after what had just happened. Again, I wished my car was any color but pink.

Twenty minutes later, which seemed like hours when one is sitting in a car doing nothing, Slater and Ricky exited the hospital and walked over to Ricky's truck. A few spaces over were Slater's truck. It took them a few minutes to load tools from one to another, and then I watched as they stood and held a conversation.

"Come on guys, quit talking," I mumbled impatiently, followed by a heavy sigh. After what seemed like an eternity, I watched as they shook hands and parted ways. "Finally." In haste, I grabbed my purse and exited my car, and headed towards the entrance.

I found Claire sitting at the end of the bed, massaging Travis's feet. She looked my way and smiled. "Hey, how did it go? How was Tilly?"

It was obvious she had been crying, and her smile was forced. She looked past me and watched the door close behind me. "Where's Ricky? Didn't he go with you?"

Whatever hostility I felt towards her soon disappeared as soon as I entered the room and was engulfed in the depressing environment of Travis's accident and Claire alone with him. "Tilly is fine, and Ricky hates me. Anything from Travis?"

"No, nothing." She gave Travis a loving smile. "He looks so peaceful. I wonder if he dreams." She creased her brow. "Wait. Did you say Ricky hates you?"

I grabbed a chair and dragged it to Claire's side, and slumped down. "Oh, I've been so stupid. I got into a huge fight with Ricky before we kissed and then again after."

Claire froze. Her eyes grew wide. "Wait back up. You two kissed, but before you kissed, you got into a fight, and then after you kissed, you got into another fight? Is that what you said? You've only been gone a couple of hours. I didn't even know you and Ricky had something going on."

"Well we don't now, that's for sure, and we probably never will." I leaned back and closed my eyes. "God, I totally blew it. It was like the old me came back for a visit. I was such a bitch to him."

Claire shook her head and then returned to rubbing Travis's feet while she talked. "I'm not following any of this, Jill. Can you at least fill me in?"

"Well, if you must know, it all started because you pissed me off and also Slater and Sabela, but I took it out on Ricky."

"What. Why were you mad at me? I wasn't even there."

"Because of what Ricky told me."

"And what did he tell you?"

"Look, this sounds stupid now. But when I was away from here and not able to see Travis and everything you are dealing with, I was angry when Ricky told me that Slater wants you and Travis to run a foster home in the house he inherited from Eve."

"You're kidding? Why would you be angry at that?"

I shifted in my seat. I realized how ridiculous I sounded. "I was upset because no one had told me. Ricky thought I already knew."

"Are you serious? You got into a fight over that? How were we supposed to tell you, Jill? You weren't exactly friendly towards us." Claire stood, pacing around the room. "And what Travis and I do is really of no concern to you. So no one told you." She raised her hands and continued to pace the room. "Big deal. What, were we supposed to seek your approval or something?"

I crouched in my seat. Claire was not hiding her anger. "Look. I'm sorry, okay. I was out of line. I realize that now. I guess the news shocked me."

"I'd say you were out of line. And why the hell get mad at Ricky? He had nothing to do with it. He is a really nice guy. I'm not sure where the kiss came in. I'm still confused over that one."

"Well, after I got mad, I stormed off and went to the gym after I left your place. Ricky was there, and he kissed me."

"And for that, you got mad at him? Yeah, I guess the old Jill came back."

"I was still upset over the surprising news about the foster home and other stuff too, and his timing for kissing me was awful. What can I say?"

Claire shook her head. "Ricky makes a move on you, which is quite flattering, by the way, and you get pissed off again at him. The poor guy. No wonder he split. I would too."

I raised my voice a notch. "Look, it's not just about the foster home. If you must know, I feel guilty about having any kind of fun while Travis is here fighting for his life. I may not be his girlfriend anymore, and you may find it hard to believe, but I still care about him, and it just seems so wrong to go have any kind of fun while he is lying here."

Claire's voice softened, and she returned to her seat. "Jill, I'm sorry. I had no idea you felt that way."

"There's a lot you don't know about me. I wasn't going to say anything, but I needed to explain myself. I know I can be a bitch at times, but I am trying to change. I guess after today, I have to try harder. Damn, and I really liked Ricky too."

Claire shrugged her shoulders, "Then go after him."

I laughed. "Yeah, right, me chasing a guy? And besides, he hates me."

"Oh, that's right. Jill doesn't chase men; they should always go after her."

"I never said that."

"You don't have to, Jill. It's pretty obvious. You've always been self-centered. I'm sorry if you don't like to hear the truth, but it's one reason why you and Travis broke up. If you are serious about changing, then do something you've never done before. Go after a guy that you really like, and might I also add, one, you also owe an apology."

# CHAPTER 16

*I* knew Claire was right, and I could kick myself now for screwing things up with Ricky. "I have no idea how to go after a guy, Claire. What would I say to him?"

Claire tossed back her head and laughed. "You are impossible. How about telling him you're sorry? It's the least you could do."

I raked my hands through my hair. "God, I don't know. What if he blows me off?"

"And what if he doesn't and accepts your apology? You'll never know unless you try."

"I don't know. I'll have to think about it for a few days."

"Well, I wouldn't wait too long. He's a good-looking guy. He might find someone else."

I needed to change the subject. "So what made you and Travis decide to run a foster home? I can't see Travis taking care of a bunch of kids."

"You didn't get to know him when you were together, did you? More than anything, Travis wants to be a dad. He wants to be a family man."

My skin tightened. "Travis wants kids? If that's the case, why don't you and he have a kid together? Isn't that easier than starting up some foster home?"

"No, Jill, it's not." Claire paused and lowered her eyelids. "You see, I can't have kids."

"You can't?"

"No, I can't, but Travis and I want to raise and have children. We want a family. Did you know Travis had a miserable childhood spending all of it in and out of foster homes?"

The news stunned me. "No, I didn't. He never told me."

"That's because you never showed interest in anything about him."

Guilt consumed me. Claire was right again. I was so wrapped up in what I wanted that I never gave Travis any attention or listened to what he had to say. Looking back, I suddenly saw how selfish I had been. "Why wasn't he adopted into a permanent home?"

"I'm not sure. Travis only knows that his birth mother was fifteen when she had him and was put into what was supposed to be a temporary foster home until he could be adopted out, but that never happened. By the time he was seven, he had become a problem child and was moved from place to place because no one could handle him. He even spent two years in a juvenile correction facility until he was sixteen and ran away from the last home he was in for a few weeks when he was released. He has been on his own ever since."

"Wow, I had no idea. Poor Travis."

"That's why he wants to run a foster home. He wants to give kids in the system a loving home—something he never received. And I would love to find his birth mother, so he has something solid about himself. I want this for him. The thought of them never knowing each other saddens me so much."

"What about the father?" I asked.

"I'm not even sure if he is on the birth certificate. I'd be surprised if they are still together. They were so young. Shit, they were just kids themselves."

"Any luck on Facebook?"

Claire shook her head. 'Nah. Just a bunch of good luck. I'm not sure now if Kent is his real name or given to him after being put into care. Oh, and I called that school, the one in Manteca."

"How did that go? Did you find out anything?"

"No, they couldn't tell me anything because I'm not a relative." Claire flopped her body back into the chair. I have no leads, just a bunch of dead ends."

"I'm sure something will turn up soon. It's only been a day."

"I hope so. I really want this for Travis."

We were interrupted by the door opening and glanced in its direction at the same time. Sabela and Slater entered the room.

Slater walked over to Claire's side and rested his hand on her shoulder. "Hey, how is it going?" he whispered. "Any news with Travis?"

Sablea leaned in and hugged me. "Hi, Jill."

"Hey."

Claire shook her head. "No changes. He hasn't moved or anything. Not even a twitch."

Slater walked over and stood by Travis' Side. "His face looks more bruised than yesterday. Is that normal?"

"Yeah, the doctor told me that would happen. It will get worse before it gets better."

"Well, he was right. It looks terrible, and the whole side of his face is swollen." Slater turned to face Claire. "How are you holding up? Have you eaten today?"

"Yeah, Jill bought me some lunch from the cafeteria."

"That was hours ago. What are you doing about dinner?" Slater asked."

Claire shrugged her shoulders. "I'm not sure. I'm not hungry."

Sabela spoke from where she stood next to me. "Claire, you have to eat. You've been here all day."

"I'm afraid to leave him. What if he wakes up? I have been talking to him, whispering in his ear—massaging his feet and hands. I'm certain he hears me and feels me. It's just a matter of time before he responds. I must be here for that."

Slater sat on the edge of the bed and took another look at Travis before looking over at Claire. "I understand, Claire, but you need to take care of yourself too. Ricky is on his way back here in about a half-hour. Why don't we all go out for a nice dinner? My treat."

My jaw dropped, and I quickly closed my mouth. "Ricky is coming here?"

"Yes, he is finishing up a job and then heading over here," Slater replied.

I quickly stood and threw the strap of my purse over my shoulder. "Oh, I have to go."

With a quick jerk of her hand, Claire reached over and pushed me back down into my chair. "Oh no, you don't."

I gave her a hard stare. "Claire, what was that for? I really must go."

"Bullshit. You are going to stay and face the music. Where do you have to go in such a hurry all of a sudden?"

Slater and Sabela gave each other a puzzled look. "Face the music? Did we miss something here?" Sabela asked.

"If I'm going to spend a few days at your place, I need to go home and get some clean clothes," I told Claire while trying to stand, but Claire quickly pushed me back down again.

"You can go after dinner. Trust me; you will thank me later."

"Can someone tell us what the hell is going on?" Sabela said as she wrapped her arm around Slater's waist. Slater pulled her in closer and kissed her cheek.

While staring at me, Claire spoke. "Jill here owes Ricky a huge apology. She needs to kiss and make up."

Slater chuckled. "I'm not sure about the kissing part."

Claire gave him a smirk. "Why not? They've already kissed once."

I slapped Claire's arm. "Claire!"

Sabela's eyes widened, and her jaw dropped. "Wait, what? Jill and Ricky have kissed. When did this happen? I haven't been gone that long."

Claire released another smirk. "This afternoon and then Jill was a bitch to him, and he stormed off." She held up two fingers. "Twice, I might add."

Sabela released a huge grin. "Is this true, Jill? You kissed Ricky?"

My cheeks turned a shade of red. "Well, if you must know. Yes, we did, and then I blew it."

"And I told Jill to go after what she wants. She says she is trying to change, but I guess she doesn't want to change that much. Jill doesn't chase guys." Claire said with a large dose of sarcasm.

"It's not that. I look like crap. I need to go home and change. My face and hair are a mess."

Claire cracked a sarcastic laugh. "Suddenly, you are afraid you look like crap for him. Quit making excuses. You look just like you did when Ricky kissed you this afternoon. He obviously likes this look on you; otherwise, he wouldn't have made a move on you. The real and natural Jill without her face caked with makeup. In fact, I do too."

I rolled my eyes. "Claire, I can't do this. I need time to prepare myself and figure out what I'm going to say. This isn't easy."

"Only because you are making it out to be more difficult than it really is." She turned and looked at Sabela. "Right, Sabela?"

"Oh yes, right. Just get it over with. There's no time like the present." She turned and smiled at Slater. "And after you do, we can all go out for dinner."

"I cringed in my seat. Oh, I don't know about this. Ricky probably hates me."

Claire looked down over her glasses. "Well, you will soon find out. He should be here shortly."

# CHAPTER 17

"Can I at least use the bathroom here to freshen up?" I said while wiping my sweaty palms across my knees.

"Sure," Claire replied.

Relieved that I would be able to make myself somewhat decent, I grabbed my purse from the floor and dashed for the bathroom. With the door closed behind me, I embraced the solitude, leaned my back against the door, and took a deep breath. "I can't do this," I whispered. After another short, deep breath, I pulled myself away from the support of the door and met my reflection in the mirror. I looked like crap. "Look at me. I'm a mess. I don't have a shred of makeup on, and what did Claire mean by caked on my face? I don't wear that much."

After routing through my purse, I found some pink lipstick and a tube of mascara. "This will have to do. I tugged at my hair with the brush I had found at the bottom of my purse. "Why the hell did I have to open my big mouth and tell Claire. I wouldn't be here shaking in my boots if I hadn't." I stopped brushing and stared at the mirror. I didn't like what I saw.

I released a loud moan of frustration. "Damn her for putting me on the spot like this." giving my hair a few more tugs with my brush. "They are all probably laughing at me out there. If they think I am going to talk to Ricky in front of them, they have another thing coming. This is between me and Ricky, not them."

After applying some mascara and lipstick, I smacked my lips and teased my hair with my fingers in an attempt to bring it back to life. It helped a little, but it was in desperate need of a shampoo and blow-dry.

"Jill, are you okay in there?" Claire called from the room.

"Yes, I'll be out in a minute," I called back, checking myself in the mirror again. I still wasn't happy with the way I looked and searched my purse one more time. Nothing, just gum and more junk that I didn't need and had no idea why I carried it around every day.

I pinned my ears and listened to the conversation in the other room, curious If they were talking about me. They were not.

"Any idea how long Travis may be in a coma?" I heard Sabela ask.

"No. According to the doctor, all we can do is wait." Claire replied, and then I heard a door open.

Slater greeted the person who had entered the room. "Hey, Ricky."

I sucked in the air and froze. "Shit, he's here."

I held my breath as I listened some more and heard Ricky and Slater exchange words.

"Are you finished for the day?" Slater asked.

"Yes, I got your tools in my truck, but I'll need them for tomorrow."

"Great. I thought we'd all go out for dinner and get Claire out of here for a while. I'm buying."

Hidden in the bathroom, I anxiously waited for his response.

"Sure, sounds like a good idea."

"Damn it!" I cussed under my breath as I folded my arms in front of me.

"We are just waiting for Jill to come out of the bathroom." I heard Claire say. I could just vision the smirk on her face as she spoke.

Ricky's voice dropped a notch. "Oh, Jill is here?"

I visioned her smirk getting bigger. "Yeah, she should be out in a minute."

Ricky spoke again. "You know what? I changed my mind. Maybe some other time. I just remembered I have to take care of some things. I'll catch up with you all tomorrow."

A few seconds later, I heard the door close. My heart dropped. "He hates me." Tears pooled in my eyes as I gathered my purse and opened the door.

All eyes were upon me as I stood in the doorway, clutching my purse to my chest. "See, I told you. He wants nothing to do with me."

They all looked at me with pity. "I'm sorry, Jill. Maybe he just needs a few days." Claire said.

I shook my head. "It's okay. It's my own fault. I Can't say I blame him. I'm just glad I didn't make a fool of myself." I took a seat next to Claire, and she surprised me by taking my hand.

"I was only trying to help. I'm sorry if I was a little hard on you. I think you and Ricky would make a great couple."

I sniffed back some tears. "Yeah, me too, but Ricky certainly doesn't. Let's get something to eat. I need to get out of here."

Over dinner, I was grateful the subject of Ricky didn't surface again. Instead, we talked about Travis and Claire, and we offered to help in any way we could. It was decided that I would stay with Claire for the next week and help her with Tilly. She planned on being at the hospital as much as possible. I planned to swing by my place and grab some clothes and whatever else I may need for a week. If Sadie weren't home, I'd text her and fill her in. More than likely, I assumed she would be with Logan.

Slater said he would come by the hospital every day after work and check in on Travis. Sabela would pick up Scottie from his grandmother's tomorrow and keep in touch via phone and be by whenever she had the chance or when Slater could stay with Scottie.

"We are all in this together, Claire," Slater said. "You and Travis are family to us, and we are here for you."

"I know, and thank you. I love you guys." she turned and smiled at me. "And you too, Jill. I'm so happy we have become friends. I never thought it was possible."

"I think it's fantastic," Sabela said and threw us both a large smile.

"I'm happy for you Claire. I never knew how nice you could be."

Claire laughed. "The feeling is mutual."

I checked my phone for the time. "Well, I should get going. I still need to go to my place, and then I think I will head over to your place and take care of Tilly. Do you want to come with me or go back to the hospital?" I asked Claire.

"I would like to go back to the hospital for a few more hours." Claire glanced across the table at Slater and Sabela. "Can you guys give me a ride? I can take a cab home."

"Of course," Slater replied with a nod.

"You will do no such thing." I barked. "I'll pick you up at ten."

"Are you sure? I hate for you to run back and forth."

"I wouldn't offer it if I minded." I stood up from the table. "I'll see in a few hours."

Claire stood and hugged me. "Thanks. I'll see you soon."

After leaving the restaurant, I sat in my car and allowed my mind to drift back to thoughts of Ricky. If he had joined us tonight, would we be leaving together right now? It was a nice thought that sadly never happened, but it made me realize I was chasing away the one thing I knew I wanted. I have no right to ask him to wait for me. Travis would want me to keep living. I needed to make it up to Ricky. I just hope it's not too late.

# CHAPTER 18

When I arrived home, I was surprised to see Sadie sitting at the kitchen table, looking at her phone. "Hey, I didn't expect to see you here."

When she looked up, I could tell from her swollen red eyes that she had been crying.

"Yeah, Logan and I got into a fight. It's our first one, and it sucks." Tears pooled in her eyes.

I took a seat across from her at the table. "Are you okay? What happened?"

Sadie wiped her cheeks. "Oh, it was just a stupid fight over nothing. He got upset because I wanted to be home tonight. I've been at his place all week, and I've been texting you with no replies and wanted to stay home so I could see you. I feel awful that I've been gone since Travis's accident, and I just wanted to make sure you were okay."

I glanced at the phone that I was holding and checked my text. There were two from Sadie today. "I'm so sorry I've not answered your texts. It's just been a crazy day. That is so sweet of you, but

I'm sorry about you and Logan. Does he know about Travis and why you wanted to be here?"

"Yeah, he knows. He texted me a few minutes ago apologizing for being so selfish."

"Well, that's a good thing. So why are you still upset?"

Sadie leaned back in her chair. "Because we shouldn't have gotten into a fight in the first place. And when I say a fight, it wasn't really a fight. When he called me to ask what time I would come over, I simply told him I wanted to be home tonight, and I'd see him tomorrow."

"And what did he say?"

"He asked me why and that he wanted to make us a nice dinner which I thought was sweet." She gave a faint smile. "He loves to cook. He's super romantic and treats me like a queen." She rolled her eyes. "Unlike my last boyfriend."

"So, what did you tell him?"

"I told him just what I told you, that I hadn't seen you in two days, and I wanted to make sure you were okay. I even invited him back here, but he said it would feel weird because it's your place and not mine." He then said, "why not go home, check on you and then go back to his place?" And when I told him he lives forty-five minutes away, and that it was too much driving, he got upset and hung up."

"What? What did he say before he hung up?"

"He said fine, and that was it. The line went dead. I tried calling him back, thinking the call had dropped, but he wouldn't pick up. At first, I was pissed at how stupid he was being, but I couldn't stop crying by the time I got home. He hurt my feelings. I've been with him all week. I have to come home sometime."

"Are you guys okay now? You said he text and apologized."

"Yeah, we will be fine. I haven't texted him back; I want him to stew for a while. There was no need for this. He wants me to move in with him. But I'm not sure I'm ready for that. It's too soon."

"Funny, I was just thinking about that the other day."

"What, that I'd move in with him?"

"Yes. You are never here anymore. I'm sure it will happen in the near future. Logan wants to be with you all the time. It's why he acted the way he did. Don't be so hard on him. I think it's kind of cute and flattering, and it shows you how much he cares about you."

"You don't think it's a little over the top? Getting upset because I wanted to be home."

"Maybe a little, but he soon realized he was wrong and is now trying to fix it by apologizing." I reached across the table and squeezed her arm. "Let it go. I know how much you like Logan. Shoot, you've told me enough times. Text him back and tell him you'll see him tomorrow."

Sadie smiled and reached for her phone. "Yeah, you are right? Thanks. But before I do. Tell me how you are doing. How is Travis?"

I stood up from the table and fixed myself a cup of herbal tea while I talked to Sadie. "We are all hanging in there. Travis is still the same. In a coma. Tomorrow will be the third day. It's tough seeing him like that, and the hardest thing is that we can't do anything but wait. I'm glad you are here, by the way. I was going to text you, but telling you in person is much better. I just came by here to grab a few things. I'm going to stay at Claire's for a week and help her out. So you will have the place to yourself, but once you and Logan make up, I'm sure you will be over there all the time."

Sadie's jaw dropped. "You are staying at Claire's? I thought you couldn't stand her?"

"I couldn't, but everything changed after seeing the accident. My heart went out to her. And the funny thing is we get along pretty good. Who would have thought? Hey, how's work?"

"It's busy. Dr. Larson called in a temp for the front desk. She is okay but slow. She's probably in her sixties."

"Oh well, then I guess I shouldn't be afraid of her stealing my job."

Sadie laughed. "Not a chance, but I sure do miss you."

"I miss you too, and I hate to rush off, but I have to feed Claire's dog, Tilly. I'm going to pack and head over there. You will have the place to yourself. Pity Logan didn't want to come over."

Sadie waved off my comment. "Oh, that's okay. I'm going to soak in the tub and have a quiet night alone with my own company. It's been a while."

I left home fifteen minutes later and was greeted by a happy Tilly at Claire's place. After taking her outside and feeding her dinner, I bent down next to the couch because something caught my eye on the floor and reached down to pick it up. It was one of Travis's photos that we were looking at last night before we uploaded some to her laptop. It must have fallen on the floor. Afraid it might get lost, I wanted to return it to the box in the dresser where we found it.

I opened up the drawer and saw Claire had put the box back exactly in the same place where we had found it. I pulled it out with both hands, turned around, and set it on the bed before putting the photo inside. I was about to return the box to the drawer when a white envelope fell where it had been leaning against the side of the drawer. I hesitated before picking it up and turned it a few times in my hand, debating whether I should open it. The front had no name, and it was unsealed. I took a seat on the edge of the bed and stared at the white envelope in my hand, contemplating what to do.

I had always been somewhat nosey and soon found myself running my fingers across the top. Inside was a folded piece of paper. I pulled it out and opened it. "Holy shit. It's Travis's birth certificate. I read it out loud. "Mother's name Caroline Kent. Father's name unknown. Claire said Travis did know his mother's name. Why did he lie?" I read some more. "Place of birth Anaheim

California" Year of birth 1988." I couldn't wait to get back to the hospital and show Claire. We now knew his mother's name. This is a huge game-changer. We finally have a lead."

# CHAPTER 19

The drive to the hospital was shortened by five minutes because of the speed I was driving. Eager to show Claire the break in our research, I raced through the corridors to Travis's room and arrived, heaving my chest.

I found Claire sitting next to Travis's bed with her head resting lightly on his chest. My heavy breathing startled her, and she quickly lifted her head. "Are you okay?"

I held out the envelope. "Read this."

Claire took it with a creased brow. "What is it?" she asked as she pulled out the single piece of paper."

"Just read it."

I watched as Claire's eyes grew wide while she read the paper. "Oh my god. It's Travis's birth certificate. Where did you find this?"

I found one of the photos we were looking at last night on the floor in the living room. I went to return it to the box, and this envelope was tucked away in the back. I hope you don't mind. But I had to see what it was. I had a feeling it was Travis's because everything else in that draw is."

Claire stood from her chair. "I'm glad you did. I can't believe you found this. We have his mother's name." She was silent for a moment. "I wonder why Travis never told me her name?"

"Had you asked him?"

Claire shook her head. "I never directly asked him if he knew her name. He told me the only thing he knew was that she was fifteen when she had him. He never mentioned her name."

"Huh. Maybe he just didn't want to talk about it." I changed the subject. "I wonder what happened to his father. He is not on the birth certificate."

"No, they normally are not if the parents are not married or if the father is not at the birth." Claire folded the certificate and slid it back in the envelope. "You know, when I was doing some research online, I saw a lot of places that will look for lost parents. I'm going to try reaching out to some of them. I have no idea what to do with this information, but they will."

"Don't they charge?"

"I'm sure it can't be that much. I'm going to send some emails tomorrow."

I checked the time on my phone and saw it was after ten. "Are you ready to go?"

Claire looked at me with sad eyes. "I'm never ready to go." She returned to Travis's side and took his hand. After raising it gently, she kissed it and then leaned in and kissed his cheek. His face was still swollen, and the bruises were now a deep purple. "I hate leaving him. I just want him to wake up so we can continue with our lives."

"I know you do, Claire. Have you spoken to the doctor today?"

Claire nodded and kissed Travis's hand again. "Yeah. They ran some tests and did another brain scan. He said that the swelling is shrinking a little, which is a good sign. He pretty much said there is nothing more they can do but wait."

"And still no idea how long he may be in a coma?"

Claire shook her head. "Nope. The doctor said everyone is

different. I'm rubbing his feet and hands every day and talking to him just like I do on a normal day. I honestly believe he can hear me, and he knows I am here."

I touched Claire's shoulder. "I'm sure he does. I'll bring you back here early in the morning."

"Are you sure you don't mind? I'm just not up to driving. I'm constantly thinking about Travis and don't trust myself behind the wheel."

"It's fine. I want to help in any way I can. But if you don't mind, I would like to go to the gym first thing. They open at 6:00 am. I want to be there at 6:30. I can come back afterward and take you to the hospital."

There was a sparkle in Claire's eyes when she spoke. "The gym at 6:30? But you always go in the afternoons, I thought." She smiled and waved her finger at me. "Wait a minute. Does Ricky work out in the mornings?"

I felt my cheeks blush. "Maybe."

"Are you going to talk to him? Is that why you are going there?"

"I'm going to try. Let me put it that way. He soon left when he found out I was hiding in the bathroom. He may leave the gym just as quickly."

"Listen, I can drive myself to the hospital. That way, you are not rushing in the morning. I had no idea you were planning to make a surprise visit to Ricky." Claire's eyes suddenly grew wide. "Hey, do you want me to talk to him?"

I suddenly panicked and raised my voice. "No, Claire, I don't want you to talk to him. Please say you won't."

"I'm sorry. No, I promise I won't. No need to bite my head off."

"I'm sorry. But I want to fix this on my own. I really like him, and I fucked things up, and it should be me that does the talking."

"You're right. Oh god, I hope Ricky listens to you. That would be so cool if you two started dating."

I laughed. "Now, hold on a second. I'm just trying to fix a broken friendship. Who said anything about dating?"

Claire nudged my arm. "Oh, come on, he kissed you."

"Yeah, and it will probably never happen again. I'm not going to lie. I would love it if he kissed me again, but shit, I need to get the guy to talk to me first. The funny thing is, I know very little about him, but man, I can't stop thinking about him and regret pushing him away. How long have you known him?"

"I've only known him a short while since dating Travis. He joined us a few times when we had lunch with Slater and Sabela. She could tell you more. She's known him since she and Slater got together." Claire nudged my arm again. "So what are you going to say to him?"

I tossed back my head and raked my hands through my hair. "Gosh, I have no idea. But whatever I decide, it better work because I don't think I'll give it another try if it doesn't."

# CHAPTER 20

That night I tossed and turned while I tried to figure out what to say to Ricky. It terrified me that he would just storm off without saying a word. I couldn't erase his gorgeous face from my mind. Why did I push him away? I'm such a fool. I relived the kiss over and over in my head touching my lips, imagining my fingers were on his lips. The thought of being held by him and feeling his hair brush against my cheek got my blood flowing. And if I weren't sleeping on Claire's couch, I would have pleasured myself to a climax while fantasizing about him making love to me.

The delicious aroma of coffee brewing in the kitchen woke me the following day. I wasn't sure what time I eventually fell asleep, but it didn't feel like it was too long ago. In a panic, I reached for my phone sitting on the coffee table and checked the time. It was 5:30. I needed to leave in a half-hour if I were to catch Ricky at the gym, which opened at 6:00. I could get there by 6:15 if I hurried. I soon realized not having to worry about putting on a lot of makeup like I used to would be a huge timesaver.

I found Claire in the kitchen with her back to me, stirring a cup of coffee. "Hey," I whispered, not wanting to startle her. "You're up early."

Claire turned and smiled. "Yeah, I need to take a shower, and I want to be at the hospital by seven. What time are you leaving?"

"In about a half-hour. Mind if I take a quick shower first?"

"Oh, go ahead. That's fine. Will you be coming by the hospital afterward? I'll be dying to hear how it went at the gym."

"Of course. I'll bring breakfast, and then I'll come back here and take care of Tilly. Wish me luck. I'm so nervous. I've never done this before. It feels weird."

Claire gave me a caring smile. "It's all part of the new Jill."

I chuckled. "Yeah, I guess."

I took a quick shower and got dressed in my workout clothes so I wouldn't have to change at the gym, packing a change of clothes in my bag. I didn't have time to blow dry my hair and shook it vigorously before running a brush through it.

"All yours," I said to Claire. I walked through the kitchen, where she sat at the table, scrolling through her phone. "I can put my makeup on out here so you can have the bathroom."

Claire looked up. "I've not seen you wear any makeup in days. I don't think you need any."

"Oh, I can't give it all up completely." I laughed. "I need help in some areas. But I do agree I like the fresher look. I hate to admit it. I did overdo it a bit. My skin feels better."

"And besides, Ricky has only seen you this way. He may not know who you are with all that gunk on your face." She joked. "Like I said, he was attracted to the fresh and natural Jill."

I nodded. "True. Okay, take your shower. I may be gone when you get out. I'll see you at the hospital."

# CHAPTER 21

*I* don't know how many times I thought about turning around and forgetting about the whole thing on my drive to the gym. I still had no idea what I was going to say to Ricky. My stomach churned as I pulled into the parking lot. Was I about to make a big fool of myself? After checking my face in the rearview mirror, I brushed my damp hair and applied some lipstick. Claire was right. Just a little mascara, lipstick, and blush were sufficient. "Okay, let's do this," I whispered under my breath as I reached for my bag, sitting in the passenger seat, stepping out of the car.

Immediately I spotted Ricky's truck parked under a shade tree. My heart raced. "He's here!" I froze to my spot, contemplating whether to go through with what now seemed like a ridiculous idea or drive off before he comes out and sees me. "Oh god, what should I do?" I scanned the parking lot. There were only two other cars. I reached for the door handle and squeezed it tight. "I don't know if I can do this." I pushed the door open and stepped out. My chest heaved, and I turned back to look at my now empty seat in my car. My heart raced, and I felt like I was about to throw up.

"Calm down, Jill. You can do this." I turned and looked at the gym entrance and then back at the driver's seat again and quickly got in my car.

After throwing my bag on the seat next to me, I fired up the motor and looked at the front door to the gym. I spoke out loud, trying to decide on what to do. "Just go in their Jill. What's the worst that can happen? So he won't talk to you. But at least you will know. If you don't go, you will never know."

My eyes stared back at me from the rearview mirror, urging me to leave my car. "Oh, fuck it. I'm going in." I grabbed my bag and purse and stepped out of the car again. Before I changed my mind, I quickly locked it and marched forward without looking back.

Nancy Was at the front desk and greeted me with her friendly smile. "Hey, Jill, you are here early."

"Yeah, I have a busy day ahead. I thought I'd sneak in a quick workout."

"Well, you picked a good time. It's always quiet this early."

"Thanks," I replied as I headed to the double doors of the gym. I stopped, gripped the handles of one of the doors, taking a deep breath. "You can do this," I whispered as I slowly opened the door and entered the large room. Only three people were working out, all were men, and it didn't take me long to spot Ricky.

He was at the punching bags dressed in black gym shorts and a t-shirt, and his hair was tied into a ponytail. How ironic. It was where we had first kissed. His back was towards me, and his punches had a fire beneath them. I stood by the door and watched —each punch and kick was thrown with massive force. He released a loud grunt every time he made contact with the bag. The bag swung hard from his hits and kicks.

Every muscle in his legs and arms was flexed and prominent beneath his tanned skin. From where I stood, I could see the beads of sweat running down his arms as they glistened from the bright lights above. He was perfect in every way, and I wanted him.

He was not aware of my presence as he continued to kick and punch the bag. Slowly, with my stomach in knots and my heart racing, I made my way towards him, still unsure what to say. When I was within a few feet, I walked to the left and stood in front of the bag.

Ricky looked up and grabbed the bag to stop it from swinging. "What do you want?" He asked in a flat tone.

"Would you rather hit me than the bag?" I said, trying to humor him.

He continued to hold on to the bag. "Don't tempt me. What are you doing here? I thought you came in the afternoons."

I set down my gym bag and purse and took two steps closer to him. "If you must know, I came looking for you."

He kept up his guard and remained rigid where he stood. "Why?" His tone was cold, and he showed no emotions.

I took two more steps. "I want to tell you I am sorry."

He remained still, his face blank, and released his hold on the bag. "Apology accepted. Now, if you don't mind, I would like to finish my workout. I have to be at work in an hour."

I stood in silence, not knowing what to say next.

"Move out of the way of the bag."

I grabbed the bag and gave Ricky a hard stare. "Can we please talk?"

He spoke with a level of sarcasm. "Oh, there's more. I thought you were done." He remained cold when he spoke. "What else did you have to say?"

I let go of the bag and inched closer to him. We were now within two feet of each other. "Can we please talk about us? That's why I came here so damn early."

Ricky creased his brow and let out a sarcastic laugh. "Us? You made it quite clear twice that there will be no us. Remember, you said you weren't ready."

"I'm sorry, okay. I panicked, and I was wrong. Why are you making this so hard?"

Ricky chuckled again. "Me making it hard. You're the one that keeps shutting me down. I'm not falling for it again. I get it, okay. I accepted your apology; what more do you want?"

I took another step closer and rested my hand on his chest. Ricky looked down at my hand and then into my eyes. "I'm asking for another chance, Ricky. Can we start over?"

My heart sank when he took another look at my hand still resting on his chest and lifted it away as he spoke. "I already tried that, and if you recall, it didn't go over too well." He released a harsh laugh, turned, and grabbed his towel draped over a nearby chair. He shook his head before wiping his brow and spoke in a flat tone without making eye contact. "I gotta go."

I watched with my heartbeat pulsating in my feet as he stormed off and disappeared through the double doors. Tears pooled in my eyes. I was devastated and confused. Why wouldn't he give us another chance? Did I hurt him that much when I blew him off after he kissed me? What should I do now? Do I walk away and ignore the attraction I have for him and pretend it doesn't exist? Is that what he is doing? If it is, then he is stronger than me. I can't let this go. I won't let this go. My fears of chasing after a man disappeared; instead, they were replaced with determination and knowing this was meant to be.

Ricky and I have something. I felt it, and I know he did too. One of us cannot give up and not let whatever we have slip away and pretend it never happened. If Ricky is not willing to, then I am.

# CHAPTER 22

My adrenaline was racing, and my head spun. I wasn't going to let him get away, and grabbed my bag before running towards the door. Nancy was sitting at the front desk. "Are you leaving already?"

I didn't look at her as I hurried to the main entrance. "Not yet," I replied as I scanned the parking lot through the window and was relieved when I saw his truck still parked under the shade tree, which meant he must be in the changing rooms. I darted back past the front desk and made a left to the men's changing rooms.

I hesitated at the door and inched it open. It sounded quiet. Being early, I hoped there would be few men inside. After pushing the door further, I leaned my head through the gap and scanned the room. From where I stood, it looked empty. I took a deep breath and entered. Holding my breath, I tiptoed through the empty room of benches and lockers and saw only one bag on the last bench. I recognized it to be Ricky's. Puzzled, I scanned the room again, and then the sound of running water caught my ear.

Behind me was a frosted glass door. I soon realized it was the shower room and set my bag down next to Ricky's. I didn't question my next move, and I just went with my gut and slowly opened the door. A mass of steam coming from the far stall greeted me. It was the only one being used. It had to be Ricky, no one else was here. My heart pounded, and my breathing increased to a pant. What was I doing? I ignored my self-questioning and tiptoed to the stall. Only a blue curtain separated me from the person in the stall, which I hoped was Ricky. Any noise I was making was being drowned by the water running in the shower.

I took a deep breath and quickly undressed until I was naked— leaving my clothes in a pile on the floor next to me. Goosebumps quickly appeared on my arms and legs from the chill, and my nipples instantly grew hard. "Here goes nothing," I whispered under my breath as I pulled back the curtain and stepped into the steamy, hot shower.

Startled by my intrusion, Ricky jolted his head. "What the fuck?" When he saw it was me, his jaw dropped as his eyes scanned my naked body from head to toe. "Jill, what the fuck are you doing?"

"What's it look like I'm doing? I want to make it up to you." Before he could answer, I pushed my body against his until I had him backed against the wall.

"Jill, this is crazy."

I gave him a hard stare and spoke with an edge, "Shut up." Before he could reply, I silenced him with my lips and kissed him hard. His body was frozen, pressed against the wall of the shower. His arms limp against his side. I forced his lips open with my tongue and engulfed his mouth with mine as I pressed my breast against his slippery wet chest. Still, he did not respond to my advances and remained still as I gave his chest a hard rub with the palms of my hands. I kissed harder and pushed my hips against his, and it was then that I felt his erection brush against my thigh. In one swift move, I took it in my hand and caressed it. Instantly Ricky responded, "Damn you." He whispered as he pushed himself away from the wall and spun me around until I was against the wall.

I had him and broke away from our kiss and lifted my head underneath the shower-head. Water splashed off my face as Ricky devoured my breasts and traced his tongue down my middle with deep, hard licks. He pulled me in closer and bit my flesh, gently teasing it with his teeth. "God, Ricky, I'm so sorry," I said between gasps. He didn't respond. Instead, he buried his face between my legs and licked me where it mattered. I moaned from the warmth of his tongue and latched on to his hair, gripping it hard as Ricky ignited every sensual nerve I owned.

He licked me hard and good as water streamed over our bodies from the warm shower, but I wanted this moment to last and pulled him away just before I was about to come. Ricky stood, his lips swollen and moist. I smiled. "My turn."

He understood and returned the smile as I knelt before him and took him in my mouth. "Oh god, Jill, you have no idea how good that feels." He moaned as I took him in deeper and engulfed his erection. Ricky pulled on my hair and held my head close to him as I worked my magic on his manhood, quickening the pace and stroking until he couldn't take it anymore, and with one quick move, he withdrew and spoke with his chest heaving. "Turn around."

I placed my palms on the tiled wall. Within seconds, Ricky was inside of me. I gasped and moaned as he thrust his hips and pushed himself deep inside of me. With his hands on my hips, he quickened his pace and pushed harder. "Damn, you feel so fucking good." He panted as he rode me harder and faster. Within minutes we both released loud, satisfactory moans as we climaxed together—both our bodies jolting in rhythm to each orgasmic thrust.

"Holy shit, woman. Are you crazy?" Ricky said as he pulled out of me. He leaned against the wall away from the spray of the water with his eyes closed.

I turned around and laughed and stroked his chest before kissing him tenderly on the lips. "Just going after what I want."

Ricky chucked and curled his arm around my shoulder and pulled me in closer. "I can't believe you came into the men's dressing room. You are one crazy lady, and I like it."

I laughed again and nuzzled against his chest. The sound of his heart beating soothed me, and I closed my eyes. This was where I had yearned to be, and it was worth going out of my comfort zone and seducing him. "I've never seduced a guy before." I laughed. "I hope you didn't mind."

Ricky ran his fingers through my hair. "You can seduce me any time you want."

I looked up into his eyes and kissed him again. "Does that mean we are good now?"

He kissed me back. "We are more than good. I'm not letting you go again. Like it or not, you are my girl now."

I smiled and kissed his chest. "I like that," I said with a smile, pulling him back under the spray of water. "I'm getting cold," I said as I wrapped my arms around his waist and allowed the warm water to run down over our skin.

Suddenly, we heard a door opening. "Shh," Ricky said. "Someone is here."

"Shit, my clothes are on the floor out there," I whispered.

Ricky pinned his ears. "I hear a curtain. They must be getting in the shower. When they turn on the water, I'll grab your clothes and bring them in here. You can quickly get dressed before they come out." Ricky turned the faucet off and wrapped me in his arms to keep me warm. Together in silence, we waited, and within minutes we heard running water. Ricky quickly pulled back the curtain and grabbed his towel from the hook on the wall and my clothes.

"Here you go."

After giving myself a quick dry with the towel, I was in my clothes in no time except for my socks and tennis shoes, which I carried in my hands. Ricky quickly wrapped the towel around his waist and took my hand as we tiptoed across the tiled floor to the door.

I waited as he peeked his head through the door. "Shit, there are three guys getting changed."

"Now what?"

He released a small chuckle. "Well, you are just going to have to walk through there like you own the place, and I'll get dressed and meet you in the lobby."

My jaw dropped. "What? They are going to know what we were doing."

Ricky laughed as he wrapped his towel around his waist. "Yep, they sure are, and they'll probably get a kick out of it." He took my hand. "Come on; I'll walk you out."

"Shit, okay." I took his hand and felt my cheeks blush as we walked through the aisle that led to the door out to the lobby.

I made sure not to make eye contact with anyone as we walked past.

"Hey," One guy said to Ricky

Ricky nodded and said, "Hey." As he walked by.

When we reached the door, he gave me a quick peck on the lips. "Let me get dressed, and I'll meet you in the lobby."

"Okay," I said before quickly exiting the room.

When I was free of the locker room, Nancy greeted me with her usual friendly smile. "Oh, you are still here. How was your workout?"

"It was one of the best ones yet," I said with a huge grin.

"Oh, that's fantastic."

I nodded and gave her another smile. "Yeah, sometimes you have to push yourself to get the results you want."

A few minutes later, Ricky entered the lobby carrying his bag and now wearing faded jeans and a white t-shirt. His hair was still damp, and he had combed it back away from his face. He threw me a brilliant smile, followed by a super sexy wink that made me blush.

I smiled back and melted in his arms when he approached me and kissed me passionately on the lips. "That was the best damn workout I've ever had." He said before giving me another warm kiss.

I looked into his soft blue eyes and giggled, "I was just telling Nancy the same thing." I glanced her way when I said her name and laughed again. Her mouth was gaped open as she looked our way and quickly diverted back to her computer when our eyes met.

Ricky continued to hold me around the waist as he spoke. "I don't know about you, but I worked up an appetite. Let me take you out for breakfast before I have to go to work."

I gave his arm an affectionate squeeze. "Sounds good. I promised Claire I'd bring her some breakfast to the hospital. I can get something to go for her from the restaurant."

Ricky grabbed my hand. "Great, I know this great mom and pop restaurant ten minutes from here."

As we walked past the front desk, I turned and gave Nancy a smile who still seemed dazed by Ricky and I displaying open affection. "Bye, Nancy. I'll see you tomorrow."

Nancy nodded and waved. "Er, sure. Have a nice day."

We stood in the parking lot, wrapped in each other's arms, and kissed once more. "I'm so glad you are not as stubborn as me and went after what you wanted," Ricky said, followed by another long, sensual kiss.

I rested my palms on his chest. "What I did was purely out of my comfort zone and something I've never done before. I don't want you to think I make it a habit of throwing myself at naked men in showers. But I blew it and wanted to make it up to you."

"And you did. I was so turned on." Ricky pulled me in tight and nuzzled his nose against mine. "I meant it when I said I really liked you. I've not been able to stop thinking about you since I first laid eyes on you. I'm not going to let you go again. Is that okay?"

I kissed him hard on the lips and found his tongue. It was long and passionate. Our chests pounded when we broke free. "Yes, I wouldn't want it any other way."

Ricky continued to breathe heavily when he spoke, still recovering from our last kiss. He glanced around the parking lot. "There she is. The pink Mustang. Can't miss it, can you?"

I gave Ricky a playful slap on the arm. "Hey, don't make fun of my car."

Ricky laughed. "It's just so bright. I'm not sure how many times we'll be riding in your car."

"I love pink. What can I say?" The sound of my phone ringing from inside my purse interrupted us.

"Damn it. Hold on." I said, fumbling through my purse, following the sound. "It's Claire."

Ricky nodded. "Tell her I said hi."

"Hey, Claire."

Claire was frantic. "Jill! Travis is twitching his toes. I was rubbing them, and I felt his big toe move. He's done it twice since then. The doctors are with him. I had to come out into the hallway and tell you real quick. They think he may be waking up."

I gasped. "Oh, my god. We are on our way."

"We? Who's we?" Claire said, sounding puzzled.

"Never mind. Oh my god, Claire. This is good news. I'm crying. I'll see you soon."

Claire broke into tears. 'It is good news. Can you call Sabela and Slater? I called my mom and dad, and I needed to go back into the room. See you soon."

"I will. I can't believe this."

As soon as I ended the call, tears poured down my cheeks. "My god. That was Claire. The doctors think Travis may be waking up. He is twitching his toes. We need to go to the hospital."

# CHAPTER 23

*R*icky's eyes grew wide. His jaw dropped. "What! Oh, my god." He grabbed my hand and began walking fast to his truck. "Leave your car here. We will take my truck."

I paused in my tracks. "Leave my car? What if it gets stolen?"

Ricky tipped his head back and laughed. "No one is going to steal a pink car."

I rested my hands on my hips as I spoke. "And why not? It's beautiful."

"Jill, think about it. Most car thieves are men. Do you honestly think they would want to be seen stealing a pink Mustang?" He took my hand and began walking fast to his truck. "Come on, enough about the car. It will be fine here. We will pick it up later. We need to get to the hospital. I'll call Slater on the way."

I nodded and picked up my pace as we hurried through the parking lot. Before I could step inside the truck, Ricky hastily grabbed a pile of papers on the front seat and threw them on the back seat, and then picked up a pile of tools off the floor and moved them to the floor in the rear cab. "Sorry, my truck is a mess. I never have passengers."

"No problem. Come on, let's go."

Once we were on the main road, Ricky talked to Slater through the speakers of the truck. "I'm not kidding, man. Claire just called us. We are on our way over there. Hope you don't mind, but Travis is more important than work."

"Wow, I can't believe this, and yes, of course, take the day off. I'm going to get Sabela and Scottie, and we will meet you at the hospital." Slater paused. "Hey, wait a second. Did you say we? Who is with you?"

Ricky glanced my way and shrugged his shoulders.

I giggled and gave him a nod

"Er, Jill is with me."

"Really. Well, I'll be. You'll have to fill me in. You guys finally made up then?"

"Yeah, I guess you could say that. I'll see you guys at the hospital."

I gave Ricky a playful stare. "Fill him in? What exactly are you going to tell him? That I seduced you in the shower."

Ricky cracked a laugh. "Well, you did, didn't you?"

I gave him a friendly slap on the arm. "Ricky, don't you dare tell him!"

As we drove through the busy street, weaving in and out of traffic, I couldn't help but wonder if Travis would be the same as the one we all had grown to care about, like family. "God, I hope Travis doesn't have any side effects." I pleaded out loud.

Ricky placed his hand on my thigh and gave it a gentle squeeze. "One good thing is that he has not been in a coma for too long. That's probably a good thing."

"Well, Claire wasn't sure if he was waking up. We'll know more when we get there."

Ten minutes later, we were pulling into the parking lot of the hospital. "Why am I so damn nervous!" I barked as I stepped out of the truck.

After locking the truck, Ricky took my hand and gave me a tender kiss on the lips. "If it makes you feel any better, I'm nervous, too. I don't know what to expect."

I squeezed his hand. "Me neither. Come on, let's go."

# CHAPTER 24

*A*fter rushing through the doors, I suddenly came to an abrupt stop. Ricky turned to face me. "Are you okay?"

"Maybe I should text Claire before we go barging into the room? The doctors might be there monitoring him."

Ricky nodded. "Good idea."

We headed over to the waiting area, where I took a seat and texted Claire. Within seconds, she texts me back. I read it to Ricky. "Doctor Ryan is here. He says it's okay if one of you comes. He doesn't want too many people in the room. Would Ricky mind waiting for a while? My parents are on their way too. He can keep them company."

"I don't mind at all. Slater and Sabela should be here soon. I'll fill them in on what's going on." He tapped my thigh. "Now go on. Claire needs you."

I leaned in and gave him a tender kiss on the lips. She giggled.

"What's so funny?"

"I was about to say I'll text you with updates, but it suddenly dawned on me I don't have your number."

Ricky echoed my laugh. "You're right."

With my phone still in my hand, he recited his number to me as I entered it into my phone and added a heart icon after his name. "Okay, I promise I will keep you updated. Gosh, wouldn't it be wonderful if he woke up and had no side effects?"

"That's what we are all hoping for."

"Yeah, I know. I gotta go." Reluctantly I let go of his hand and headed towards the hallway that would take me to Travis's room. In her last text, Claire hadn't told me whether Travis had any more signs of waking up. For three days, we have waited for this moment. I can only imagine the emotions Claire is experiencing right now. Unsure of what to expect. Praying Travis will be his usual self, and they will continue with their lives. And what if he is not? I shook my head. I didn't even want to have those thoughts.

When I approached the door to Travis's room, I took a deep breath and knocked lightly. I heard footsteps from inside walking towards the door. It opened slowly, and Claire stepped out into the hallway, closing the door behind her.

"Hey. How is he doing?" I said in a soft voice.

Tears ran down her face, and she fell into my arms. Jill, I'm so scared. What if he doesn't know me, or he can't talk or remember anything? I just want him to be okay. I want my Travis back."

I soothed her with soft rubs to her back as I spoke. "I know, Claire. I'm scared too. But Travis is a strong man and a fighter. We have to think positively and tell ourselves that he will pull through."

Claire pulled away and stood up straight. She wiped her face with her palms. "After I spoke to you, I went back and continued rubbing his feet and talking to him like Doctor Ryan told me to. His toe twitched again, and the doctor started speaking to Travis, asking if he could hear him. But there was no response." Claire lowered her head. "He hasn't moved since."

"Can I come in?" I asked.

"Yes, of course. I want to keep talking to him. Maybe you can too. He knows your voice."

I released a sarcastic laugh. "The sound of my voice may prevent him from waking up. He may not want to."

Claire gave my arm a friendly slap. "Oh, stop it. Come on, let's go in."

When we entered the room, the doctor entered some notes into his tablet and looked up when he heard us.

"Any more news, doctor?" Claire whispered.

"No. His vitals all look good. I've scheduled a scan in the morning to check the swelling on the brain. I am expecting to find a substantial decrease. In the meantime, keep talking to him. Massage his hands, arms, and feet. Let him know you are here waiting for him. Any more changes, call for a nurse. If I'm still here, they will call me."

"Thank you, we will."

After doctor Ryan left, Claire took a seat next to Travis and kissed him tenderly on the cheek before talking to him in a soft voice. "Hey, Travis, we are back. Jill is here, and we are not going anywhere until you wake up."

I took a seat on the other side of the bed and took Travis's hand. "That's right, Travis. We all miss you."

Claire continued to rub his palms and stroke his hair as she spoke to him about Tilly. I noticed his face was looking much better. The bruising had faded to a light yellow and a little darker around the eyes. His left cheek was almost back to normal, and his lips were no longer purple. His nose was still a little bruised, but a lot of the swelling had gone down. Little by little, Travis was returning to us.

I remained quiet, holding Travis's hand while I listened to Claire pour her heart out to Travis and the love she had for him. It was beautiful to witness. They had a passion I had never experienced. Ricky suddenly popped into my head, and I let go of Travis's hand when I realized I had not texted him in over an hour with any updates. I pulled out my phone and sent him a text letting him know there were no changes.

Claire glanced my way. "Who are you texting?"

"Ricky. He is in the waiting area." My phone pinged again, and I read the text. "Slater and Sabela are there too with Scottie." I looked up. "I've never met their son."

"Oh, he is the cutest little boy and so polite. Looks like Slater's mini-me." Claire joked.

I laughed. "Really. I can't wait to meet him. Your parents are there too."

"Yes, they texted me earlier." Claire quickly changed the subject. "So you came here with Ricky?"

I nodded. "Yes, I did."

"In his truck?"

I smiled. "Yep."

Claire matched my smile. "So I guess you guys made up."

I felt my cheeks blush. "We sure did, and it was so friggin hot. I'll tell you all about it later."

Claire's eyes grew wide. Her jaw dropped. "Oh my god, you had sex with him."

"Claire! Now is not the place."

"Why not? It might wake up Travis," she joked.

"I'm not saying anymore, but damn, it was good."

"I'm happy for you. See, you went after what you wanted and won. I'm so excited. You guys make a great couple."

"Thanks. If it weren't for you telling me to go after him, it would never have happened, so thank you. I still don't know much about him, but damn, the sex was good."

Claire laughed. It was good to see her smile. "That's the fun part. Getting to know each other."

"It sure is." I glanced at my phone. "You know I should go back to your place and let Tilly out. She needs dinner too. Will you be okay for an hour? It would give everyone else a chance to visit with Travis."

"That's a good idea. My mom and dad are eager to see him."

"Yes, and Ricky can take me back to the gym to pick up my car."

Claire creased her brow. "You left your car at the gym?"

"Yes." I leaned in and whispered. "It's where we had sex. I seduced him in the shower."

"Wow, Jill. When you go after a guy, you don't mess around."

"I couldn't help myself. He was like a magnet." I quickly stood from my chair. "Okay, enough about my sex life; I'm going to go meet little Scottie and tell Ricky he is coming with me. I'll be back as soon as I can. Call me if there's any news."

"Will do."

I found the rest of the gang sitting in the waiting room, and a young boy I assumed was Scottie knelt in front of the table playing with some cars and making motor noises with his rolling lips. Claire was right; he was Slater's younger version. "Hey, guys," I said as I approached the seating area.

Slater stood and gave me a friendly hug. "Hey, Jill. Any news?"

"I shook my head. No. he is still in a coma. No more movement, but his face is looking much better. Doctor Ryan has scheduled a CAT scan for tomorrow morning to check on the swelling on his brain." I walked over to his son and smiled. "This must be Scottie."

Sabela ran her fingers through Scottie's charcoal color hair. "Yes, it sure is. Say hi, Scottie."

Scottie looked up and gave me the cutest smile only a child could give. "Hi."

"I've heard a lot about you, Scottie. It's so good to meet you finally."

Scottie had already returned to his world of cars and nodded. "He's adorable. Claire was right. He looks like you, Slater."

"He sure does," Slater replied.

I glanced over at Ricky and smiled. He had my heart. "Hey, I need to go feed Tilly. Can you give me a ride?"

"Where's your car?" Sabela asked.

"At the gym."

"So, how did you get here?"

Ricky stood and walked over to me. He took me in his arms and kissed me tenderly on the lips. "I gave her a ride."

The looks on their faces were priceless. Sabela gasped and raised her hand to her mouth. "Oh my goodness. Are you two dating?"

Ricky looked into my eyes and smiled. "Jill, are we dating?"

I laughed. "I sure hope so."

"Oh, I'm so happy for you guys." Sabela squealed. "I've wanted to introduce you two for a while now, but with everything that has happened in the last few months, I've not had the chance. You guys are perfect for each other. Congratulations." She turned and smiled at Slater. "Can you believe this? Jill and Ricky are dating."

"I think it's fantastic. Now we just need Travis to wake up and celebrate with us."

"How is he?" Claire's mom asked.

"He is still the same, but the doctor thinks he may wake up soon. Claire said you guys could go back there." I turned and looked at Slater. "Do you mind letting her parents go first?"

"Not at all. We will Take Scottie to the cafeteria for a snack, and you and Ricky will be able to take off."

I laughed. I was back in the circle. I had missed it, and now wrapped in Ricky's arms, I felt complete.

# CHAPTER 25

When we stepped into Ricky's truck, and before he had even closed his door, he pulled me in close and pressed his body up against mine, and kissed me passionately on the lips. I melted instantly and wrapped my arms around his neck and closed my eyes. The kiss was long and sensual. Our tongues mated, and we panted while we kissed.

He pulled back and looked into my eyes. "Man, I love kissing you. Your lips taste so sweet."

I found myself lost in his gaze, and when he brushed my cheek lightly with his fingers and then swept my hair back away from my face, my skin tingled, and my heart fluttered with lust. He was perfect in every way. I leaned back in the seat and closed my eyes. Ricky's warm breath masked my face. He kissed me again. This time he caressed my breast through my light pink t-shirt, causing me to moan. I arched my back and welcomed his touch. "God, what are you doing to me?" Ricky whispered. He left my lips and traced my neck with his tongue. "Every time I'm near you, I want you."

My chest heaved as I spoke. "I want you too. This is incredible."

Ricky lowered his head to my chest and kissed my breast through my top. "I can't get enough of you. Even when I was mad at you, I couldn't stop thinking about you." His hand traveled down between my legs, and I parted them and raised my hips.

He gave me a hard squeeze on my groin, and I gasped. "I want you, Ricky."

Our lips met again in a passionate state. Our tongues explored, and the adrenaline raced through our bodies. Ricky continued to tease me through my spandex Capri pants, using deep, circular massage rubs over my crotch area. My hips circled to the rhythm of his hand. "God, Ricky, whatever you are doing, don't stop."

Ricky rubbed harder and used more force. I gasped and engulfed his mouth to silence my orgasmic screams. "Jesus!"

Ricky didn't stop. He engulfed my cries with his lips as my body lost control and embraced the orgasm.

When my heart rate finally subsided and my breathing slowed, our kiss became less animal and more sensual. "Wow! Where the hell did that come from?" I said, followed by an embarrassed giggle. "I don't think I have ever come so fast and with my pants still on." I laughed.

"That was frigging amazing. If we weren't sitting in this parking lot, I would have ripped off those pants and been inside of you so damn quick." He gave my breast a gentle squeeze. "Something to look forward to," he said, followed by another long, drawn-out kiss. "Come on, let's get out here before I have my way with you."

I smiled and nuzzled up to his chest as he fired up the truck and draped his arm over my shoulder. I loved his masculine scent and breathed it in as Ricky pulled out of the parking space and drove to the exit. "You know, it just dawned on me. I don't even know how old you are."

"Does it matter?" Ricky chuckled.

I matched his chuckle. "No, but it would be nice to know. There is a lot I don't know about you."

"Well, I could say the same about you. I have no idea how old you are and know very little about you either."

I sat up and rubbed his thigh. "Okay then. I'm twenty-seven years old. I have never been married. You probably already know that Sabela and I used to work together. I'm an only child. I was spoiled rotten by my two-attorney parents that I never saw when I was growing up. They were too busy working or traveling the world, and now they live in Spain. I last saw them five years ago before they left. I'm fine with them leaving. I never really knew them anyway. They feed their guilt by sending me big checks at Christmas and the once-a-year phone call on my birthday." I paused to think of anything to tell him. "Oh, I love the color pink."

"Really, I would never have guessed." Ricky smirked."

I threw him a cocky laugh. "Haha." I slapped his thigh. "Okay, it's your turn."

Ricky took a deep breath. "Okay, let's see. I'm twenty -four."

My jaw dropped, and I couldn't hide my reaction. "You're younger than me. I've never dated a younger man."

"Is that a deal-breaker?" Ricky joked and shook his head.

"Not at all. I kind of like it."

"Shall I call you my cougar?" Ricky joked.

"No!" I shrieked. "What else should I know about you?"

Ricky thought for a moment while watching the road ahead. "Let's see. I, too, have never been married. My mom and dad divorced when I was twelve. Dad moved to Florida, where he now lives with his second wife, and he is also in construction. My mom never remarried but has had a boyfriend for the past eight years. They live in New York, where he owns a brewery which she helps manage. I have a sister, her name is Annie, and she is two years older than me. She lives in Los Angeles, and she is shacking up with some guy who doesn't work. The last I heard, she was a wait-ress by day and a bartender by night. We make the occasional phone calls, but we're not close. I last saw her about three years ago when mom and her boyfriend Tony came out for a visit and helped find Annie a place after she graduated college. Ricky released a sarcastic laugh. "A lot of good that did. She got a degree in journalism and ended up being a waitress."

"So, how did you end up working for Slater?"

"I met him and Sabela on a job." Ricky laughed. "Let me rephrase that. I caught them making out on the job. It was so embarrassing. Back then I was just a kid and very shy. Later on, when Slater was working at Eve's house, he called my boss Drew, asking if he could send some help his way. I gladly volunteered, and I've been working for Slater ever since. Drew is fine with it. I live in the area, and Drew is now building condos over an hour away. I'd much rather work close to where I live. I told Drew I'd always be happy to help if he comes back this way."

"That's the house Slater wants to turn into a foster home, right?"

"Yeah, he's hoping that Travis will make a full recovery. He's not giving up on the idea. He wants to do it, and he knows how much it will mean to Travis and Claire, seeing how they can't have kids, and Travis was fostered. He wants to give back. I get that."

"Oh, you know."

"Oh yeah. We all had a serious conversation about it over dinner a while back when discussing plans for the house. I have great admiration for the two of them. God, I hope Travis can run the place."

"Yeah, me too. I'm just finding out about all of this. When Travis and I broke up, I treated them both pretty badly. I blamed Claire for everything even though Travis and I hadn't gotten along in months."

"Really. I would never have guessed. You and Claire seem to get along great. What changed?"

"I hate to say it, but Travis's accident brought us together. I no longer feel rage. Instead, my heart went out to Claire, and I just want to be there for her."

Ricky pulled me in closer and kissed my cheek. "That makes

sense. I've heard of people experiencing life-changing events. It looks like you did."

"Oh, I definitely did. I could never go back to the old me. I was such a bitch not just to Claire but Travis too, and I'm sure I was to Sabela a few times also." I glanced out the window. "Make a left here, and her condo is the third building on the left."

After Ricky put the truck in park, I stepped out and led him up the steps.

"I don't live too far from here. I have a one-bedroom apartment just a few miles away." Ricky told me.

"We are all so close to each other. I'm only about fifteen minutes away."

"Is that the place you used to share with Travis?"

"Yeah. I have a roommate now, Sadie, but I think she will be moving in with her boyfriend soon."

"Then what will I do? Get another roommate?"

I turned the key in the lock to Claire's condo as I spoke. The familiar bark of Tilly sounded on the other side of the door. "I'm not sure yet. I'll cross that bridge when I come to it." I pushed on the door, and Tilly bounced through the doorway. "Hey, Tilly."

Ricky laughed as he watched her run from one end of the hallway to the other. "Feisty little thing, isn't she?"

"Yeah, she's been cooped up all morning. Hey, do you want to take to her for a walk in the park? It's just across the street."

"Sure. I'd love to."

"Great. Let me grab her leash. It's hanging on the back of the door."

It was the perfect day for a walk. The skies were blue with no clouds, and there was a slight breeze in the air. The leaves of the trees rustled as we walked the trail hand in hand. "I love that sound. When the light wind blows through the trees," I said, looking up to the swaying branches.

Ricky gave my hand a tight squeeze. "I'm enjoying this. The last time I took a dog for a walk was junior high when we had a family dog named Sam. He was a black Labrador."

"Me too. We had a dog growing up. Her name was Molly. She was a Golden retriever, but I've never had one since I've been on my own, but since I've been taking care of Tilly, I've been thinking about getting a puppy."

"Really."

"Yeah, I have. Maybe another Golden retriever." I shook my head. "It won't happen anytime soon. But I think it will happen. I had forgotten how much fun dogs are." I pointed to an empty bench. "Do you want to sit down for a while? I can let Tilly off the leash and let her run around."

"Sure."

Once Tilly was free from her leash, she immediately ran circles around an oak tree. Ricky and I laughed from where we sat on the bench. His arms draped over my shoulder, and my head rested in the crook of his neck. "Hmmm, you smell good," I whispered before giving him a light kiss on the side of his neck.

Ricky hugged me and kissed the top of my head. "You feel good in my arms. It feels so right."

I turned my head and gazed into his eyes. A sense of belonging was present. Our lips met, and the kiss was long and passionate. "I have to tell you, Ricky, but I'm falling for you pretty hard. If that scares you, now's your chance to run."

Ricky kissed me again, but this time with a little more force. "I'm not going anywhere. You are stuck with me. If you must know, I've fallen pretty hard for you too. I find it mind-boggling that it's only been half a day, but I cannot imagine my life without it. You have become a part of me that quickly."

Tears pooled in my eyes. "Ricky, I feel the same way. I can't imagine a day without you in it. I think it's amazing, and I haven't been this happy in a long time."

"Me neither."

Suddenly, my phone dinged from inside my pocket. I pulled it out and glanced at the screen. "Shit! It's Claire. Travis is showing more signs of waking up. His fingers moved, and so did his toes again." I jumped up from my seat. "Come on; we have to get back to the hospital."

"Oh shit! Let's go."

After calling back Tilly, we hurried back to Claire's condo, fed her, left some lights on, and then raced to Ricky's truck.

Ricky fired up the truck and then turned to face me. It was then he noticed the tears flowing down my cheeks. "Hey, are you okay?"

I leaned in and buried my head in his chest. "I'm scared. What if Travis has severe side effects? Or, even worse, don't recognize any of us. I don't think I can handle it."

Ricky cradled me in his arms. "Hey. We have to think positively. We have to believe that he will be fine, but no matter what, he is still our friend Travis, and we will be there for him no matter what."

"I know, but what if he can't speak or walk?" I rattled my head from side to side. "I'm scared to death that he might be physically scarred in some way."

Ricky gave my shoulders another squeeze. "And if he is, then he and Claire will need our help even more, and we will be there for them no matter what." Ricky freed his arm and put the truck in gear. "Let's be there for them both when he wakes up, okay?"

I nodded and wiped my eyes. "Okay."

# CHAPTER 26

$\mathcal{W}$e arrived at the hospital in record time. Slater and Sabela, plus Scottie, were in the waiting area, huddled together in two seats. Scottie sat on Slater's knee, and he had Sabela cradled in his arm.

"Hey guys, how is he?" I whispered when I noticed Scottie was asleep.

Sabela raised her head and looked my way. Her red eyes told me she had been crying. "Doctor thinks he is slowly waking up. At first, he thought the toe movement was a nervous twitch, but now he is moving some fingers."

I took a seat next to Sabela, and Ricky sat next to Slater. "Did he say how long it would take for him to fully wake up?"

Sabela shook her head. "He has no idea. Everyone is different." Tears trickled down her cheek, and she brushed them away with her hand. "God, I can't stop crying. What if he is not the same? I don't know if I can handle that."

I covered Sabela's hand with mine. "I know. I lost it in Ricky's truck and bawled my eyes out. I have the same fears. But Ricky reminded me we have to stay positive not only for Travis but for Claire, too. How is she, by the way?"

"She's hanging in there, but she's scared too. More than us, I'm sure. She was holding his hand when she felt his pinky twitch. We were in the room with her and we immediately called a nurse. Doctor Ryan was there within ten minutes. He's evaluating the situation now. Claire said she would text with any more news or if any of us can go back into the room. Her parents are with her right now."

I glanced over at Scottie and saw he was still asleep in Slater's lap. "Hey, do you guys want to head home? Scottie looks beat. I'll call you the minute there is more news."

Sabela looked over at Slater. "Do you want to go home, sweetie?"

Slater looked down at Scottie and nodded. "Yeah. He'll be needing lunch soon after he wakes up." He gave me a stern look. "You promise to call right away?"

"I promise. Ricky and I aren't going anywhere."

After they left, I texted Claire to let her know we were in the waiting area. She immediately texted me back and said I could come to the room. Her parents were going to head home for a while. They are exhausted. "Oh wow!"

Ricky quickly sat up. "What is it? Is everything okay?"

"Oh, yes. Claire asked me to join her. I wasn't expecting that."

"Well, why are you still here? Go."

"Are you going to be okay out here?"

"I'll be fine. Just let me know if there are any changes."

After giving him a soft kiss on the lips, I stood, grabbed my purse, and headed down the hallway. I wished Ricky was by my side; I needed someone to hold on to as I walked down the desolate hallway, unsure of what lay ahead. With my clammy hands shoved in the pockets of my jacket, my head spun with horrific images of Travis unable to speak or walk. I wanted to be rid of the uncertainty I was feeling; Travis is going to be okay, I kept telling myself repeatedly, but the images kept haunting me.

A nurse passed me. She nodded and smiled, and I smiled back. The only noise was coming from my head. I was frightened about the future. For Claire and Travis. Was her head tormenting her like mine? I turned down the hallway where Travis's room was and took a deep breath. My feet dragged as I approached the door and pinned my ear to the wooden surface. There was silence on the other side.

I hesitated before knocking lightly and heard the shuffle of feet from inside the room approach the door. The door handle turned, and I took another deep breath as I found myself face to face with Claire. She looked tired. Her skin was pale, and her makeup no longer existed.

I gave her a weak smile. "Hey, how are you doing?"

Claire opened the door wider, allowing me to walk in. "Hey. I'm hanging in there."

Her parents stood and walked towards me. We gave each other a weak smile before embracing.

"We will leave you two alone," Abigail said before taking her husband's hand. Call us if there is any news."

Claire hugged her parents. "I will, mom. Drive safe."

After they had left, I scanned the room. It was dark except for a soft light next to the bed. Travis's bruising on his face had faded to a light yellow, and the swelling was almost unnoticeable. "His face looks much better," I whispered. "Any more movement?"

Claire took a seat next to the bed and held Travis's hand. She kissed it tenderly and held it up to her cheek. "No, not for the past hour. The doctor will be notified immediately if we see any changes."

"Do you plan on staying here tonight if there are no changes?"

Claire looked surprised by my question. "Well, yes, of course. I couldn't bear to be away from him for a minute. I'd be devastated if he woke up and I wasn't here. I want to be the first thing he sees, and I want him to know who I am."

I gave her another weak smile. "I'm sure he will. I'll stay with you. I don't want you going through this alone. Ricky is in the waiting area. He wants to stay too."

"Thank you. How's Tilly? I miss her."

I dragged a chair across the room and placed it next to Claire, and sat down. "She is fine. Ricky and I took her for a walk in the park."

"I'm so happy for you both. I knew you would make up. You really like him, don't you?"

I felt my cheeks blush. "I do. I love everything about him, and we get along really well."

"Do you think it could be serious?"

"Oh gosh, this might be too premature for me to say anything. We only started officially dating this morning, but between you and me, I'm in it for the long haul. I love being with him, and I love everything about him."

Claire gave me a teary smile. "Oh, Jill, I hope so too." She smiled and changed the subject. "Do you want to know what I did earlier today?"

"Yes. What did you do?"

"I emailed some companies that I found online that help you look for lost family members. They help fostered and adopted children find their biological parents."

"Oh wow! Have you heard back from anyone?"

"No, not yet, but I've also decided if they find something, I won't pursue it any further without Travis's permission."

"So you are going to tell him?"

"Yes, I have to. What if he doesn't want to meet his parents?"

"Claire, this is hard to ask, but it needs to be said. What if Travis is unable to give you permission?"

"What do you mean?"

I took her hand and looked at her with pity in my eyes. "Claire, we have to be prepared that Travis may wake up differently with side effects. His speech may be impaired, or other physical aspects may be scarred."

Claire pushed my hand away and jolted up from her chair. "I won't think of those things, Jill. I have to believe he will return just as I remember him. Perfect in every way. It's what keeps me sane and gives me strength. If I start having those horrible thoughts, I'll just collapse and go crazy."

Guilt swept through me. "I'm sorry. I didn't mean to upset you. I guess I'm just preparing for the worst."

"Well, don't. Okay." Claire snapped. She shook her head in frustration and sniffed back some tears. "I'm sorry. I didn't mean to snap at you. I'm just so stressed out."

"It's okay. I shouldn't be thinking the worst. You are right." I quickly changed the subject. "Hey, have you eaten anything today?"

Claire shook her head.

"How about I get us some lunch from the cafeteria? I'll eat mine with Ricky and then bring you something."

"That sounds good, thanks."

After leaving the room, I joined Ricky, who looked pleased to see me and a little concerned. "Is everything okay?"

"Yeah, Claire hasn't eaten, and nor have we. I told her I would get her something. Do you want to grab a bite to eat?"

Ricky rose from his seat and met me with a flirtatious kiss. "Sounds good to me. Travis is still the same?"

"Yeah, and I told Claire I'd stay with her all night here at the hospital if need be. If you want to go home after lunch, it would be fine. I hate the idea of you just sitting in the waiting area all day and maybe into the night." I had a sudden thought. "I really need to get my car, though."

"Tell you what, after lunch, I'll drop you off at your car, and then I'll probably go home until I hear from you. I may go to work. I need to keep busy." Ricky said.

"That's a good idea. After we eat, I'll take Claire her lunch and tell her I'll be back within the hour. God, all this running around is wearing me out." I joked. "I'll probably have to go feed Tilly later too."

I arrived back at the hospital in my car around four in the afternoon and would head over to Claire's in a few hours to feed Tilly. Claire hadn't texted me, which told me there were no changes. I had received two from Ricky, though in the past half hour telling me how much he misses me already. I giggled at his text and typed back how I was missing him, too.

I found Claire in her usual spot next to the bed, holding Travis's hand. I glanced over at the empty food containers and was pleased to see she had eaten all her lunch. "Hey, any more movement."

"I felt his pinkie move again about thirty minutes ago. I started talking to him straight away and kissed him lightly on the cheek a few times. But nothing since. The nurse just left."

"Okay, well, after I've taken care of Tilly later, I'm coming back here and staying with you for the rest of the night."

Claire smiled. "Thank you for all your help."

"You don't have to thank me. I'm happy to help."

For the next few hours, Claire and I whispered to Travis about anything that came to mind. She massaged his feet while I held his hand. I talked about my newfound friendship with Claire and how surprised he will be when he wakes up. I told him we all missed him, and Claire spoke about Sabela and Slater's visit and that little Scottie came too. We told him about the weather and Tilly's walk in the park.

After returning from taking care of Tilly, I had stopped and gotten us a couple of salads and milkshakes, which Claire greatly appreciated, and through the night, we sat by Travis's side, whispering to him and pleading with him to wake up. The night nurse came by twice and left us both a few blankets and a pitcher of water.

Sometime during the night, we must have dozed off, but the sound of Claire's voice calling my name and her tears woke me. "Jill. Jill. His eyes are open."

I stirred in my chair and heard my name again. "Jill. Get up." Travis's eyes are open.

# CHAPTER 27

*I* opened my eyes and focused, remembering where I was. I saw Claire leaning over Travis. "Travis, can you hear me?" She turned and looked my way. "He just opened his eyes. Find a nurse. Hurry," she whispered with force. "He just closed them again."

I remembered the red button on the wall and raced over to it and pushed it hard. It lit up, and I pushed it once more to make sure it stayed on. It did. "What time is it?" I asked Claire before I released a yawn and rubbed my eyes.

"I think it's around four in the morning." She took Travis's hand and rested it on her lips. "Travis, can you hear me? It's Claire."

I echoed Claire's words. "Travis, can you hear us?"

We watched for any expressions or movements on his face.

"Look, his eyes are twitching."

Claire repeated herself. "Travis, it's Claire. I love you, sweetheart. Can you hear me?" Suddenly she looked down at her hand holding Travis's. "His hand just twitched." She looked at me with wide eyes and whispered. "I think he is waking up. Travis, honey, can you open your eyes?"

"Where is the nurse?" I looked over at the red button and saw it was still red and then heard Claire cry. "Oh my god. His eyes are opening." Claire leaned in closer to Travis and whispered softly. "Travis. It's me, Claire."

I took a few steps back away from the bed and watched from a distance. I didn't want to be the first one Travis saw. It must be Claire. My jaw dropped when I watched Travis slowly open his eyes. He blinked a couple of times and looked directly into Claire's eyes. Tears pooled in my eyes as I held my hands over my mouth.

"Oh Travis, can you hear me? It's Claire." She lifted his hand and kissed it softly. And then an amazing thing happened, and I gasped. I watched without blinking as Travis dragged his hand away from Claire's and raised it to her face. Tears streamed down her face as Travis gently stroked her cheek and whispered her name. "Claire."

Claire cupped his hand and held it to her cheek. "Oh, Travis, you said my name. "I love you, honey."

Travis blinked his eyes a few times and slowly turned his head from side to side. "Where am I?"

Tears continued to flood her eyes. "Travis, you can speak. You've been in a coma because you were in a car accident. You are in the hospital. Do you know who I am?"

Travis's voice was weak when he spoke. "You are my love, Claire. I was in a car accident?"

Claire leaned in and laid her head on his chest. "My god, you know me. Yes, I am your love. I will always be your love."

A nurse entered the room and interrupted the momentous moment. I jolted my body away from the end of the bed and rushed to the nurse. "He is awake. His eyes are open, and he is talking." I said with excitement as I grabbed the nurse's arm.

The nurse quickly approached the bed. "Travis, I am Brenda. Can you hear me?"

Travis nodded his head slowly. "Yes." He said in a whisper.

Nurse Brenda glanced over at Jill and me and then looked at Claire. "I'm afraid your friend will have to leave for a little while until we assess his condition. The night doctor is on his way."

Claire turned her head and looked my way. Pity filled her eyes. "I'll call you as soon as I can. I'm sorry."

"It's okay. I'll be in the waiting area."

When I reached the isolated waiting room, I immediately texted Ricky, Slater, and Sadie to give them the good news that Travis was awake, speaking, and recognized Claire. It was almost five in the morning, and I wasn't expecting anyone to reply right away, but as I was finishing the last text to Sadie, my phone dinged. It was Ricky. I read the text. *That's amazing! I'm on my way. See you soon.*

"What he's coming here at this hour," I whispered under my breath.

I quickly texted him back. *"Ricky, you don't have to come at this hour. No one can go into the room right now. The nurses and doctors are with him. Only Claire can be with him. I am waiting in the lobby."*

A few minutes later, he texted me back. *"All the more reason for me to come—to keep you company. I miss you. I want to see you and kiss you. I'm in my truck. I'll see you soon."*

A smile smeared across my face when I read his sweet message. "He misses me," I whispered.

The sound of the automatic front doors opening caught my attention while I was scrolling Facebook on my phone. I turned my head and saw Ricky race between the two doors. He was dressed in faded jeans and a red and black plaid shirt. He wore loafers with no socks, and his hair looked super sexy uncombed. I stood to greet him and fell into his arms. "Thank you for coming."

Ricky held me tight and kissed me passionately on the lips. "You think I'm going to let you sit here in the middle of the night alone." He looked into my heavy eyes. "You look exhausted."

I rested my head on his chest and enjoyed the feel of his hands stroking my hair. "I am. I think I only got an hour or two of sleep before Travis woke up."

"And he's talking?"

I looked up and gazed into his beautiful eyes. "Yes. He is only whispering. His voice sounds weak, but he knew who Claire was and called her my love. It was the sweetest thing I have ever seen. Poor Claire couldn't stop crying."

"That is wonderful news. Did he know who you were?"

"I don't think he was aware that I was in the room. I stood away from the bed and let Claire talk to him. As soon as the nurse arrived, she kicked me out."

Ricky nodded and kissed me again. "That makes sense. They have to check him out before we can all see him."

My phone dinged, and I pulled it out of my jacket pocket and glanced at the screen. "It's Slater. They have to take Little Scottie to kindergarten, and then they will come here. He's stoked about the news," I laughed.

When Ricky and I sat down next to each other, I leaned in and rested my head on his shoulder. His arm draped over my shoulder. Within minutes, I was asleep and didn't wake up until I heard Ricky's voice.

After sitting up and rubbing my eyes, I saw he was on the phone. He had it on speaker, and I recognized Slater's voice on the other end. A few minutes later, he hung up.

"Oh shit, what time is it?" I said, pulling my body to an upright position and stretched my crooked neck.

"Almost six-thirty," Ricky replied. "That was Slater." He was just checking in. They just got up and are getting Scottie ready for school.

"I have to go to Claire's and take care of Tilly. Do you want to go?"

"Sure. We'll take my truck. I'm sure Claire will text us when she has more news."

I cracked a laugh. "One of these days we are going to take my car. You can't keep avoiding it."

By the time we arrived at Claire's, there was still no news from her, so Ricky and I spent some time with Tilly, who was more excited than her usual self. After taking her for a long walk and feeding her a good breakfast, Ricky made us some coffee while I took a quick shower.

"If we were at your house, I'd jump in the shower with you," Ricky called as I left the room.

"I'd be dragging your ass to join me if you didn't." I laughed.

Unsure how long we'd be at the hospital, I dressed in comfortable pink sweats and a matching top. I gave my hair a quick brush and decided to go fresh with just a touch-up of my lips with some pink lipstick.

I found Ricky on the patio with Tilly in his lap while he scrolled through his phone. "Aww, look at her. She sure is a friendly little thing. I'm going to get myself a dog someday."

Ricky looked up and smiled. "I heard your phone ding a couple of times. It might be Claire. I didn't want to root through your purse."

"Oh shoot," I said as I raced to my purse, sitting on the couch, and searched for my phone. The first text was from Sadie, who was now at work and checking in. She ended her text by letting me know she and Logan are good now, and making up last night was fantastic. "Good to know, Sadie," I mumbled under my breath.

I checked the second message. "Yes, it's from Claire," I called, making my way back out to the patio.

"What does it say?"

I read the message out loud. "Travis is doing really well. I'll tell you more when I see you. You and Ricky can come to the room."

Ricky jumped up and took me in his arms. "That is great news. Come on, let's lock up and head over there. Text her back and tell her we will be there soon."

Within a half-hour, we were back at the hospital. It was a little after nine, and Slater and Sabela hadn't arrived. "Come on, let's go straight to the room. I'm sure Slater will text one of us when he gets here." I said, grabbing Ricky's hand.

When we reached Travis's room, I knocked gently and heard Claire's voice on the other side. "Come in." Unsure of what to expect, I held Ricky's hand tight as I turned the knob and entered the room. I was shocked to see Travis sitting up with his legs dangling over the side of the bed.

Claire, who was holding Travis's hand, turned her head and gave us a huge smile. "Hey, guys. Can you believe this?"

"Oh my god, Travis, you look amazing."

"Wow," Ricky said after my surprising outburst.

Travis gave a weak nod. Claire helped him lay back by supporting his leg and swinging them gently on the bed.

I continued to hold Ricky's hand as we approached the bed. Travis looked up and spoke softly. "Hi, Jill. So Claire told me you two are friends now. I had to ask her how long I had been asleep."

I gave Travis a caring smile. "I saw the accident from my car in the parking lot. I have never been so scared in my life. When Claire came out screaming, my heart went out to her. It brought us together. I can't tell you how happy I am to know you are going to be okay.

Travis glanced down at Ricky's and my hands, which were still in a hold. "And I guess you two are an item now?"

Ricky released my hand and pulled me in. "Yeah, we sure are. So good to see you, man. You had us worried there for a while."

"Man, so much has happened." He looked at Claire. "Are you sure I was only asleep for three days?"

Claire beamed another smile and laughed. All the worry and stress she had been feeling had disappeared. Only happiness shined through her eyes. "Yes. Only three days, sweetheart." She turned and looked at Ricky and me. "Travis is doing good, but he has a long way to go. The doctors were with him all morning. The swelling on his brain has gone down ninety percent, and he doesn't seem to have any serious side effects. They had him walking within an hour, and yes, he is slow and weak, but he did great. He also complained of some ringing in his ears, which is normal, and it should fade over time. They will be transferring him to the rehabilitation ward here in the hospital tomorrow morning. He will be there anywhere from two to four weeks, depending on his progress. The main thing is to get his strength back and, of course, keep a close eye on him. And he will be on seizure meds."

"Oh Claire, this is wonderful news. It brings tears to my eyes." I glanced over at Travis. "We were so worried about you, Travis. It's so good to have you back. If there is anything I can do, I'm here for you."

"Thank you. I told Travis how much you have been helping and that you've been staying with me and taking care of Tilly. He couldn't believe it." Claire chuckled and stroked Travis's cheek with his fingers and spoke to him. "I love you so much. I will be here every day taking care of you, and when I go back to work, I'll be here after work."

"I'll continue to watch Tilly as long as you need me to. Are you staying here tonight?" I asked.

"Yes, I think so."

"Maybe I can take Tilly to my place. Would that be okay? I would like to go home tonight."

"That's a great idea. Thank you."

I turned to Travis and rested my hand on his shoulder. "It's so good to have you back, Travis. Everyone has been so worried about you. I want to tell you how sorry I am for the way I had been treating you and Claire. I'm really happy for you guys." I broke into a smile. "You got your real deal, Travis. Claire is an amazing lady and friend. I love both of you guys very much."

Travis looked stunned by my words. "Are you sure you didn't bang your head too?" He joked in a quiet voice.

"Oh, I can see you didn't lose your sense of humor." I laughed.

Travis smiled. "Thank you, Jill. It means a lot." And then he threw another joke. "I just didn't think I'd have to almost get killed for you to see what a great gal Claire is."

"Oh, stop it, Travis." Claire butted in. "I'm sure she would have come around, eventually."

"Yeah, in a million years," Travis said with a cheeky grin. "I'm sorry. I don't know why, Jill, but I have always loved giving you a hard time. I guess I still do."

I nodded. "True, you always have." I gave Ricky a loving stare. "And now Ricky does. He won't even ride in my car."

Claire let out a loud laugh. "It's pink. I don't blame him." She looked at Travis. "Did you ever ride in her car?"

"Hell no."

It was Ricky's turn to let out a cocky laugh. "See. It's not just me. You never told me Travis would never ride in it either."

I knew I was beaten. "Okay fine. I won't make you ride in my car."

Ricky turned and smiled at Travis. "Thank you, bro. You just saved the day."

"My pleasure, man. Hey, I'm really happy for you guys. When I get out of here, dinner is on me."

"Okay, we are going to leave you two alone. Do you want anything from the cafeteria? I'm starving." I asked Claire.

"A cup of coffee would be good and maybe a bagel."

"Sure, I'll bring them after we've had some breakfast." I smiled at Travis. "So happy to have you back, Travis. Like I told Claire. We may not be a couple anymore, but I consider you both family."

# CHAPTER 28

While we were eating breakfast, Slater texted me. He and Sabela were in the lobby.

"Tell him to come here and have breakfast with us. Then, give Claire and Travis some time alone." Ricky said.

"Good idea," I replied, texting him back.

Ten minutes later, Slater and Sabela walked into the cafeteria and spotted us right away.

"Hey, guys. How is Travis?" Slater asked as they both took a seat."

"Incredible!" Ricky answered. "He is sitting up and talking. The doctors even had him walking around the room."

"That is fantastic." Sabela cried. "When will he be able to go home?"

"Not for at least a few weeks," I said, picking up my coffee. "It all depends on his progress. But, first, they need to build up his strength."

"Oh wow. How is Claire doing?" Slater asked.

"She is over the moon and so happy. It looks like he will have minimal side effects, is what the doctors told Claire. I haven't said anything to her, but I'm not sure if he'll be doing construction work anytime soon."

Slater nodded his head in agreement. "You are right about that. In fact, I'm not sure if he'll ever be able to get back into the business. He'd have to have a long talk with his doctor before that happens."

"What about the foster home?" I asked.

"Yeah, I need to talk to Claire about it. I'm not going to rush her. Her priority is nursing Travis back to health. The house is always going to be there. And if it ever happened, I'd only want those two to run it. It's because of their history why I suggested the idea to them in the first place. They could give so much to the kids, with Travis being in foster care and Claire not able to have kids of her own. It just seems so perfect, and they were in tears when I asked them."

"I think it's a wonderful idea," Sabela said as she stroked his arm. "It's one of the reasons why I love you. Because of your big heart."

"Yes, and when Travis is home and doing better, we will discuss it some more with him."

After feasting on a Swiss omelet, I turned to Ricky sitting next to me and rested my hand on his knee. "I'm going to go pick up Tilly and take her back to my place. I miss my home and will probably spend the night there." I gave him a flirtatious smile. "What are you doing today?"

Ricky glanced across the table at Slater. "Hey, do you need me today?"

"We have that job on Jackson Place that needs to be finished up today. Then, after that, Jill can have you for the rest of the day," he laughed.

I matched his laugh. "Thanks, Slater."

Ricky leaned in and gave me a quick smooch. "I'll text you when I'm done and be sure to text me your address."

I stood up from the table and smiled. "I will," giving Slater and Sabela a smile. "We'll get together soon, okay."

Slater nodded. Yes, I want us to all have a big dinner with Travis when he is home with Claire. A celebration."

≈

After picking up Tilly, I quickly stopped at the store and bought a nice big slab of salmon and the fixings for a green and bean salad. I wanted to fix Ricky's dinner and probably seduce him too; I chuckled to myself. I can't remember the last time I cooked for a guy. Travis ate out most nights for the last six months we were together. I can't say I blame him. Although looking back, I wouldn't want to have eaten with me either.

I felt good about Ricky and me, and I want to show him tonight just how much. Sadie had texted me again to tell me she probably wouldn't be home for the rest of the week, which meant Ricky and I would have the place to ourselves. I smiled at the thought.

He came into my life when I was at my lowest and didn't give up on us when I pushed him away twice. Any other guy would not have given me a second chance, let alone a third, after the way I had treated him. I'll never push him away again. I've not felt this good in a long time. Even when I am not with him, I can't stop thinking about him.

I came to a stop at a red light and laughed when I looked at the empty seat next to me. I pictured Ricky sitting there, riding with me in my pink mustang. What kind of faces would he pull? Would he cover his face so as not to be seen? I laughed out loud at the thought and then flashed back to just a week ago when I felt lost and lonely. I was envious of everyone's relationships around me. Slater and Sabela. Travis and Claire. Logan and Sadie. Now, look at me. I'm a new person with a new boyfriend that I am crazy about. It's only been a few days, but it feels like I've known him forever.

# CHAPTER 29

When I walked into my home, I felt at ease and leaned against the back of the door. "I'm home." I sang with a smile and tossed my overnight bag on the couch before freeing Tilly from under my arm. "Now, don't you go marking furniture with pee, young lady," I called to her as she began sniffing the new smells in the room.

Outside, the sun was shining; the air was still, and it was a comfortable sixty-five degrees. "You can go outside on the patio when you have to go to the bathroom," I said to Tilly as I unlocked the patio door and left it open.

While Tilly continued to get acquainted with her new surroundings, I freshened up and changed before Ricky arrived. I stayed with the fresh look, which I now liked much more than spending at least half-hour applying all the makeup I used to wear. My skin felt lighter and fresher, and I couldn't believe how much time I saved by not sitting in front of a mirror smothering my face with creams, foundations, and blushes. In my bathroom, I looked down at the pile of cosmetics sitting on the counter in baskets. I hadn't realized how much money I would be saving too.

After spending twenty minutes deciding what to wear, I stood in front of the mirror wearing a pair of jeans and a loose-fitting white top with spaghetti straps and opted to spend the afternoon barefoot.

Ricky arrived a few hours later, and my heart melted the minute I opened the door.

"Hey." I smiled while using the door for support.

He beamed at me with a big, sexy smile and took me into his arms to kiss me. "Hey. Did you miss me as much as I missed you?"

"I missed you more."

He kissed me again. "Wanna bet on it?"

I threw my head back and laughed. "No, I'll let you keep your money." I took his hand. "Come on in. I'm going to cook you dinner, and then we are going to make love all night long."

"I love a woman that tells me what she wants, just like in the shower."

We stood in the living room, our arms wrapped around each other's waist. "It's all your fault. I've never been this forward with a guy. But when I'm with you, I just can't get enough of you."

My neck tingled when he raked his fingers through my hair and brushed my skin with his fingertips as he pulled it away over my shoulder. "You know, we can skip dinner and eat later."

"How hungry are you?" I whispered.

He leaned in and kissed me passionately on the lips. My eyes closed, and I melted beneath his touch. "Dinner can wait but having you cannot." He whispered back before kissing me again.

I reached up and locked my arms around his neck as I forced my tongue into his mouth, which he gladly welcomed. "I agree dinner can wait. Let me show you the bedroom."

Ricky's breathing increased as he gazed into my eyes and began kissing my neck. "Lead the way, pretty lady," he said between kisses and soft, sensual licks on my neck and shoulder.

I took his hand and smiled. "Follow me."

Holding his hand, I led him upstairs to my bedroom and opened the door.

"Oh no, your bed is pink. There is no escaping it." Ricky laughed.

I gave his chest a friendly slap and giggled. "I like pink. What can I say?"

Ricky walked over to the bed and sat on the fluorescent pink quilt. "I've never made love in a sea of pink before. "It may bring out my feminine side." He joked.

He sat on the edge of the bed with his legs apart. I entered his space, and his knees cupped my legs. "You are too much of a man to be affected by a little pink." I laughed as I rested my arms on his shoulders and kissed him.

The kiss was soft and sensual. While we kissed with our tongues mating, I felt the grip of Ricky's masculine hands grab my hips and pull me in. I gasped and came up for air. Ricky jerked my body even closer until my chest smothered his face. "Damn, you smell good." He moaned as he reached up under my delicate white top and caressed my breast.

I closed my eyes from his touch and arched my back. "And your hands feel good. They are so warm."

Ricky responded with deeper massages to my skin and slowly raised my top to bare my stomach and chest. He traced his tongue down my middle. My heart raced, and my senses were on fire. "Your skin is perfect." He whispered before raising his mouth to my now hard nipples.

I gasped from his touch and bit my lip. "Oh my god, you have no idea how good that feels." I moaned as my hips swayed, and I pressed my body as close as I could to his.

"You like that?" Ricky whispered between gentle nips.

I squealed from his touch and pressed my chest harder against his face. "Yes." In one swift movement, I raised my arms, pulled off my top, and threw it to the ground. Ricky looked up into my eyes and pulled my lips onto his. We kissed hard as he leaned back onto the bed and pulled me on top of him.

Still wearing my jeans, I straddled him and pulled his t-shirt up above his head and away from his body. For a moment, I was still as I traced his defined abs with my hands. "God, you are perfect," I whispered as I lowered my lips onto his chest. His skin was well tanned—his chest smooth. He cupped my head as I left light kisses across his stomach and chest. His chest tightened, and he suddenly grabbed my shoulders and kissed me hard while he flipped my body onto the bed. So I was now lying beneath him. I cupped his neck and pulled his lips into mine. "Make love to me," I whispered.

Ricky pulled himself up and sat on the edge of the bed to remove his pants. I stroked his back while he did and then laid back and unbuckled my belt. Ricky turned and smiled, kissed my breast, and then focused on my jeans. After unzipping them, I wiggled my body as he slowly slid them down my legs and over my feet. With one final pull, my legs were free, and I immediately grabbed him by the waist and pulled him on top of me. We met in a fiery, passionate kiss and explored each other's bodies with our hands. Our moans were loud, and our chests heaved. "I want you." I gasped as I parted my legs to take him.

Ricky didn't hesitate and kissed me harder as he entered me, and I parted my legs some more so I could take all of him. Once inside of me, he rode me gently at first while not leaving my lips. The circular motion of my hips matched his rhythm, and with the rising rate of our hearts, Ricky rode me quicker and harder until we both came, and he collapsed onto my chest and into my arms with sweat beading on his forehead.

My chest heaved from beneath him, and my breathing was heavy. Finally, I was able to say only one word. "Wow!"

Ricky laughed between his deep breaths. "I agree. Damn, that was good." He looked up and kissed one of my breasts. "Did we work up an appetite?"

"We sure did. I'm starving. Let's go fix dinner and check on Tilly."

Ricky pulled himself off of me and sat on the edge of the bed. "I could get used to this."

"Get used to what?"

"Coming here, making love to you, and making dinner together."

I rested my chin on his shoulder and wrapped my arms around his waist. "Well, Sadie is at Logan's for the rest of the week, and probably the weekend, too. So why don't you stay here?"

Ricky turned to look at me. His eyes were wide. "Really? I may never leave."

I gave him a loving smile. "You know something? I don't have a problem with that."

# CHAPTER 30

*A*fter checking in with Claire the following day, our plans had changed. She was doing so much better now that Travis was awake with minimal side effects and would spend as much time as she could working with him in the rehabilitation ward. So between us, we decided there was no sense in me staying at her place. "Do you want me to keep Tilly at my place for a few weeks so you can spend as much time as possible with Travis?" I asked.

"That's a great idea. I promise to come by and visit with her. I don't want her to forget me."

After ending the text, I looked over at Ricky from the couch where I sat. He was shirtless, only wearing his jeans with his back facing me, pouring a cup of coffee. I admired his butt and how well his jeans shaped it perfectly. God, I am a lucky woman; I thought to myself as I found myself like a magnet drawn to him and left the couch.

With my arms wrapped around his waist, I nuzzled my head in the crook of his neck. "Looks like I'll be moving back home. Claire is doing much better." I glanced around the kitchen. "Going to be pretty lonely though with Sadie not here."

Ricky turned to face me and kissed the ridge of my nose. "Want some company?"

I smiled. "I thought you'd never ask."

$\sim$

I n a matter of days, everything about my life had changed. Claire and I had become friends. I stopped wearing makeup, and my favorite new word was fresh. I met and fell hard for Ricky, and I was actually liking myself. I woke up every morning in a good mood and a smile when I saw Ricky lying next to me. I've had sex every morning and night for the past four days. Ricky and I have been living like a married couple, and I was sorry to see it come to an end.

Sadie would be home in a few hours. "You don't have to leave. I'm sure Sadie would be fine with you being here." I whined as I watched Ricky pack his bag in the bedroom. "After all, this is my place."

"I know that, but I'm a nice guy. I don't want her to be uncomfortable. This is her home too."

I cracked a laugh. "She's never here." I released a moan. "I don't want you to go."

With a piece of clothing still in his hand, he walked towards me and rested his hands on my shoulders. "You can always come to my place." He looked around the room. "It's not as nice, and there is no pink."

I shook my head. "No, I had a hard time spending just a few nights at Claire's. I want you here with me. I'm going to talk to Sadie." I shook my head. "I still don't know why I need to, though. Like I said, this is my place."

Ricky lifted my chin with his two fingers until my eyes met his. "Because it's the right thing to do. It's what the new Jill would do."

I knew he was right, but I still didn't like it. "You're right. I'm going back to work tomorrow. When will I see you?"

"Well, if Sadie is cool with everything, I'll come back Monday night."

I beamed him a smile. "Really. I'm going to the hospital after I've swung by here and taken care of Tilly."

"Fine, I'll meet you over there. Text me when you are on your way." He leaned in and kissed me.

"I've gotten used to you being here. I'm going to miss you."

"Me too. I've almost forgotten where my place is." Ricky laughed.

Reluctantly, without letting go of his hand, I walked him to the front door and spun around and pressed my back against the door to block him. "Are you sure you have to go?"

Ricky chuckled and stroked my cheek. "It's just one night. I'll see you tomorrow. If you want, we can have phone sex tonight."

I slapped his chest. "Ricky!" I moved away from the door. "Go on, get out of here. I'll talk to you tonight."

His eyes lit up. "Does that mean we have a phone sex date?"

"Ricky, stop." I kissed his lips. "Now go on, go before I drag you back upstairs."

He laughed. "What kind of threat is that?" He put one foot outside the door. "I miss you already."

"I miss you too. Bye."

# CHAPTER 31

*I* couldn't believe how far Travis had come in just three weeks. I sat off to the side, watching Claire do leg exercises with him in the rehabilitation ward at the hospital. Claire was so dedicated to Travis and aiding him in his recovery every step of the way. She had not missed a day since the day of the accident, which was almost a month ago.

His strength was slowly coming back, and last week the ringing in his ears had finally disappeared. Claire walks with him for an hour every day around the grounds when she visits after work, and she has dinner every night with him in his room. I watched as Travis rode the cycle machine. "You are doing good, Travis," I called from my seat.

Claire smiled. "He sure is. Doctor Ryan said he could probably go home in a few days."

I beamed her a huge smile. "That's wonderful, Claire. Did you just find out today?"

"Yes, when he came by this afternoon. It's going to be so good to have you home, honey. I hate sleeping alone."

"I can't wait for either, babe," Travis said as he continued to peddle. "I won't miss this place, that's for sure."

"I'm going to be taking more time off work, too," Claire told Travis.

Travis looked surprised. "You are? Why? I'll be fine."

"No, you can't be left alone for a while. You are at a high risk of having a seizure. Doctor Ryan told me you shouldn't be alone for at least six weeks."

"Six weeks! That's ridiculous. You can't take that much time off from work?"

"Well, I'm not letting you out of my sight. I'll figure something out."

I pulled out my phone. "I have to text Ricky and tell him the good news that Travis is being released tomorrow."

"Where is he?" Claire asked.

I smiled. Every time I think of Ricky, I break out into a smile. "At my house cooking dinner. I told him I was going to swing by here on the way home. He got off early. Slater is waiting for the inspectors to come."

"Is he living with you now?"

I laughed. "He never left. Well, he did for one night when we first started dating, when Sadie was on her way home. I told Sadie about him and that he would hang out at the house sometimes. She was so happy for me and didn't care at all. She really likes him. Ricky came back the next night and has been there ever since. It's like we are married." I laughed.

"It sounds pretty serious. It's good to see you happy." Claire said.

Travis turned and faced me. "I agree. Ricky is a good guy. It's been a long time since I've seen you this happy, Jill."

"Thanks, Travis. I am happy." I made a sad face and pouted my lip. "Oh no, it just dawned on me you'll want to take Tilly home."

"Yes. I've missed her. You've had her for over three weeks."

"I know, and I've grown attached to her. She is so sweet, and she loves to cuddle on the couch."

Claire laughed. "You're not keeping her."

"I know, but I've gotten used to having a dog around."

"Then get one. They are the best company."

"Hey, what about me?" Travis chirped from the bicycle.

"Okay, Tilly's second." Claire joked.

My phone dinged, and I glanced at the screen. "It's Ricky. I read his text out loud. He says great news. Let's celebrate. I'm going to call Slater."

"Yes, Slater suggested we all go out to dinner once Travis is home. Do you feel up to it, honey?" Claire asked Travis.

"Heck yeah. I've been cooped up here for almost a month eating hospital food."

"Great. I'll let you know what Slater says after Ricky talks to him." I glanced at the time on my phone. "I should get going in a bit. I don't want Ricky to burn dinner. When did you want to pick up Tilly? I'm working all day tomorrow, and so are you, Claire."

"How about in a couple of hours after we've had dinner in Travis's room. That way, I can get her settled in at home before Travis arrives."

"Aww, so soon," I said with a sad face.

"Jill, you are making me feel bad about getting my own dog." Claire laughed.

"I know. I'm just giving you a hard time. But, yes, a couple of hours is fine. We'll be done by then." I picked up my purse from the floor, walked over to Claire, and hugged her. "I'll see you in a bit." I turned and patted Travis's shoulder. I'll see you soon, Travis."

"Yeah. See you soon. Thanks for coming by."

I came home to the aroma of chicken baking in the oven and Ricky swaying his hips to an Elvis song playing from the Bluetooth speaker. When he saw me enter the kitchen, he grabbed my hand and pulled me closer. I kissed him on the lips and locked my arms around his neck as we jived to Elvis. Coming home to him would never get old.

"Dinner smells good."

Ricky playfully bowed his head. "It will be ready in fifteen minutes, my lady. Can I get you a cocktail while we wait?"

I laughed at his humor and played the role. "Why would that be delightful? I will take a glass of white wine."

Ricky twirled me around. "Coming right up, my lady."

As soon as I took a seat at the table, Tilly jumped into my lap. "Aww, I'm going to miss you, little girl."

Ricky poured a glass of wine and set it on the table. "What do you mean? Where is she going?"

Claire is picking her up in a few hours. "I've gotten so attached to her, and I'm going to miss her. I knew it was temporary, and I wasn't expecting to keep her for this long, but how can you not fall in love with her." I picked Tilly up and kissed her face. "She's so dang cute."

Ricky stood before me and patted Tilly's back. "Yeah, she is a cutie, alright. I've gotten used to having her around, too. The good thing is you can go visit her whenever you want."

"Yeah, but she's Claire's dog." I looked up and gave Ricky a smirk. "I need a dog."

Ricky laughed. "I think you do."

After a delicious meal cooked by Ricky and a few more glasses of wine that I shouldn't have had, I reluctantly began gathering Tilly's things together. Tilly followed me like a shadow, wearing a worried look on her face as I put her food bowl and toys in a bag. When I grabbed her lease off the counter, she instantly began barking and jumping around in circles. "No, Tilly, we are not going for a walk. Your mommy is coming to pick you up soon." I said in a soft voice.

Claire was her usual punctual self and arrived at my place exactly two hours after I had left the hospital. After doing the dishes, which he insisted on doing, Ricky had gone upstairs to take a shower. Tilly immediately recognized Claire and circled around her legs, barking and jumping.

Claire knelt and picked her up in her arms. "Hey girl, I've missed you." She said with a huge smile as Tilly smothered her face with licks.

"Aww, she sure loves you," I said as I watched the two reunite, even though Claire was just here a few days ago, visiting with her for an hour.

"Yeah, she's my baby girl. Thanks so much for taking care of her."

"Oh, anytime. I'm going to miss her." I said, patting the back of her head.

"Oh, Jill, stop." She laughed. "You are making me feel guilty. You can come to see her any time."

"Thanks, I probably will. You might get sick of me." I joked. "I'll be at your place to see your dog, not you and Travis."

Claire cracked a laugh and then released a heavy sigh. "It's going to be so good to have Travis home. But, he still has a long way to go. He doesn't realize it, and I know the hardest part will be making him take it easy. He has always been such a busy, strong guy that worked twelve hours a day with tools and heavy equipment. But he won't be able to do that for a long time. In fact, I'm not sure if he will ever be able to return to construction."

"Have you mentioned any of this to Travis?"

"No, not yet. It's too early. I've already talked to work, and they are fine with me taking two weeks off. Thank god we have an understanding boss. But after that, I'm not sure what we are going to do. I don't think Travis should be left alone, and it will drive him nuts stuck in the apartment all day. The doctors don't want him driving for at least two months."

"It will all work out. Don't think so far ahead. You have many people around you guys who are willing to support you and help in any way they can. Including Ricky and me."

"I know. I'm a planner. What can I say?"

"Hey, have you talked to Travis about looking for his mom?"

"I did—last week. I've just not had a chance to tell you. I'm sorry."

Her answer surprised me. "You did! What did he say? Did you tell him you've hired a company to do the footwork?"

Claire set Tilly on the floor. "We had a great conversation about it. It went much better than I expected. I first told him how scared I was when he was in a coma and that the thought of his birth mother never meeting him upset me. So I explained to him how I confided in you that I wanted to look for her and that you had told me about the old photos in a shoebox and then I told him how we came across his birth certificate, and I asked him why he told me he knew nothing about his mother. I hated to ask him because he was lying in a hospital, helpless, and I'm drilling him questions. But it was all part of the conversation about his mother, and I needed to know."

"What did he say?" I said anxiously.

"He didn't say anything at first. He just shrugged his shoulders, and I asked him again if he was going to tell me. After a few moments of silence, he finally told me that when he had first told me about his mother giving him up that he didn't want to be asked a bunch of questions about her and figured it would be easier if he said he knew nothing."

I nodded. "Yeah, that makes sense. So did you tell him you've hired a company to look for her?"

Claire bit her lip. "Not exactly."

"What does that mean?"

"Well, I asked him if he would ever consider looking for her. Especially after what happened to him."

"And?" I said anxiously.

"Well, he didn't say no. He just said I wouldn't know where to start. And when I told him that maybe I could help in some way, he didn't object, and I left it at that."

"So what if this place you've hired finds her?"

"The company can't guarantee any results, and it all takes time. I'm not expecting to hear from them anytime soon in the future. If they happen to find her, then Travis and I will have another talk."

"Wow! I want to be there if his mother is found. Can I?"

Claire chuckled. "We will see when or if the time comes. Now I need to get my baby girl Tilly home. I'll call you tomorrow about dinner tomorrow night. "

"Okay, sounds good." I picked up Tilly and hugged her. "I'm going to miss you, girl." She placed her in Claire's arms.

# CHAPTER 32

After Claire left, I flopped onto the couch nearby and wiped away a few tears. I told myself I wasn't going to cry when Tilly left, but she failed. I looked at my empty lap where Tilly had always made her space when I sat here, and then I glanced over at the corner where her bed and toys had been.

Lost in my sadness of missing Tilly, I was startled when I felt a hand on my shoulder. "Hey are you okay?"

I looked up and managed a small smile when I saw Ricky standing next to me, smelling like Irish Spring soap, with only a white towel wrapped around his waist.

"Yeah. Claire picked up Tilly. I'm feeling a little sad."

Ricky sat on the arm of the couch and cradled me in his arms. "Come here."

I pressed my face against his bare chest. It was still damp and smelt fresh. "Oh, I'm being silly. I knew I would have to give her back someday."

Ricky kissed the top of my head and rocked me in his arms. "I miss her too. Let's curl up on the couch and have movie night. It will help take your mind off her."

I looked up and gazed into my eyes. "I would like that." Suddenly, I heard a ding on my phone. "That might be Claire. She might have forgotten something." I glanced around the room for my phone and saw it had slid off the couch onto the floor. I picked it up and saw it was a message from Sadie.

"It's Sadie," I said. My jaw dropped as I read her message. "Oh, my god!"

"What? Is she okay?" Ricky asked, alarmed by my outburst.

"Holy shit! She's in Vegas with Logan. They got married." I jumped off the couch and reread her message. "You've got to be fucking kidding me. She got married!"

Ricky's jaw dropped, and his eyes doubled in size. "What. No way!" He laughed loudly. "They eloped to Vegas?"

"Yep, that's what she says. And then she wrote. We are here until Sunday." I held the phone up to Ricky, who stood behind me, reading Sadie's message over my shoulder with his arms around my waist. And look, she ended it, Mrs. Sadie Ryder." I fell back onto the couch, shaking my head. "I can't believe they got married. I guess I just lost a roommate."

Ricky sat beside me and cuddled me in his arms. "Well, I'm here. I'll keep you company like I have been doing."

I leaned in and rested my head on his chest. "Dang, in less than an hour, I lost a dog I had gotten attached to and my roommate. Let's put on a movie before I get depressed again."I chuckled.

The following day, our phones were going crazy with text messages while getting ready for work.

"What the hell is going on?" I yelled from the bathroom where I had just gotten out of the shower and heard the phones ringing.

Ricky called from the bedroom. "They are from Sabela and Claire." The phones dinged again. "And another just came in from Slater."

Still wrapped in a towel, I joined Ricky in the bedroom. Is Everything okay?"

Ricky nodded. "Yep. The news is Travis will be home by ten,

and we are all going to celebrate at Leo's Bistro tonight at seven."

I released a cheer. "That's fantastic—what a way to start a day. Oh, I'm so happy. Travis is going home. Claire must be beside herself."

I reached for my phone, sitting on the end table. "I have to text her. Shoot, I wish I didn't have to go to work." I moaned as I texted her a happy text and told her I couldn't wait to see her and Travis tonight. I looked over at Ricky, who was slipping into his jeans. "Wanna meet here and drive together? I'll have to come home and change."

"Sounds good," he said as he pulled a black t-shirt over his head and shook his hair, and then sat on the edge of the bed to put on his socks and shoes.

"You're moving fast. Are you running late?"

Ricky pulled on the last shoe and quickly stood. "Yeah, I have to take care of a few things and need to leave work a little early."

"Okay. But you'll be back here in time to ride together, right?"

"Oh, yeah." He leaned in and gave me a loving kiss. "I'll see you tonight."

My excitement grew throughout the day for the celebration dinner for Travis. I can't remember the last time we all ate together. All day long, we had all been texting each other back and forth, sharing our happiness for Travis's recovery. Even Travis joined in on Claire's phone, and then he texted us all from his own. Finally, Claire let us all know when they were home and that Travis would be resting until dinner tonight.

After work, I made no stops and went straight home, so I had enough time to pick something out to wear and get ready. When I pulled into the driveway, I was surprised to see Ricky's truck. He normally showed up around six. So it wasn't even 5:30.

"Hey, Ricky," I called as I entered the front door. He was nowhere to be found. "Ricky?" I called again as I tossed my purse on the couch. I heard a sound from upstairs and looked up the stairway. "Ricky, is that you?"

"Yes, it's me. Give me a second. Don't come up," he called from upstairs.

"Okay," I said with uncertainty. Wondering what he was up to now. I waited at the bottom of the stairs to greet him. I had missed him and wanted to be held in his arms and kissed by his lips.

I heard footsteps and Ricky's voice. "Close your eyes."

I creased my brow. "Close my eyes? Why?"

"Just close them."

I giggled. "Fine." And closed them tightly. I waited and pinned my ears. "What are you doing, Ricky?"

His voice was closer. "Keep them closed."

"They are closed."

I felt his presence and smelt his cologne. "Okay, you can open them now."

Slowly I opened them, unsure what I would see, and then I gasped. Before me stood Ricky, holding a beautiful Golden Retriever puppy. Tears pooled in my eyes and ran down my cheeks. "Oh my goodness, Ricky. Is she ours?"

Ricky came down to the bottom of the steps and put the beautiful puppy in my arms. Of course, she is ours. I want you to meet Maggie, or maybe you want to call her something else?

I wrapped my arms tightly around her and nodded as I squeezed her and smelt her puppy breath. "I love the name, Maggie. It suits her. Oh, Ricky, I can't believe you did this." I gazed into her blue eyes and smiled. "Hi, Maggie. You are the cutest thing ever."

Ricky came over and stood beside me and laughed when Maggie covered my face with puppy kisses. "I saw how upset you were when Tilly left, and you were right. You needed a puppy."

"And you remembered Molly, my old Golden, and that I may get another Golden."

"See, I listen to you. How do you like the pink collar?"

I gently gripped the collar with my fingertips and rubbed the pretty leather collar to inspect it. "We need to get her a name tag.

Oh wait, does she have one?" I said, feeling something dangling from the collar.

Ricky looked at me and smiled. "Take a look."

I moved back Maggie's fur so I could see her collar better. "Ricky, what's this?"

"What does it look like? It's a ring." Ricky gazed into my eyes and kissed me softly. "I want to marry you, Jill. Maggie wants that too."

"Oh, my goodness. A puppy and a proposal in one day. I don't know what to say."

"Jill, I love you. I love everything about you. Since I have been here for the past few weeks, I know that I never want to leave. You, me, and Maggie, we are family. Will you marry me?"

"Oh Ricky, I love you too. I want to see the ring."

Ricky laughed. "Why if you don't like it, you won't say yes."

"No, I want to try it on." I looked into his eyes and kissed him. "I want you to put it on after I say yes."

"Oh, Jill, you have made me the happiest man in the world." He reached for Maggie's collar while I still held her and unbuckled it. "Hey, girl. Can I have that ring you have been holding for me?" After he had re-buckled her collar, I set Maggie down and stared into Ricky's eyes as I held out my hand. "I would love to marry you."

Ricky held up the ring. "I hope it fits. I measured it against one of your rings I took from your jewelry box."

"You stole one of my rings." I joked. He slowly slid it onto my finger. "Oh Ricky, it's beautiful, and it fits perfectly," I said as I held it up to the light and admired the single diamond with a cluster of smaller ones surrounding it. "I love you so much."

"I love you too, Jill."

"Oh, tonight we have two celebrations—Travis's road to recovery and our engagement." I took his hand. "Come on, let's get ready," I said as I called Maggie, who already seemed to know her name, and followed us upstairs.

# CHAPTER 33

"Come on, Ricky, we are going to be late," I called from the kitchen where Ricky had thought ahead and closed off an area with baby gates for Maggie. He had thought of everything for her. She had a soft bed, lots of toys, and a no-spill water dispenser. Her faint cries tore at my heart as I set her down in her area. "I'll be back soon, sweetie." She looked at me with her beautiful blue eyes and cried some more. "Oh, Maggie, you are killing me, sweetie." I leaned over the gate and kissed her snout. "You are so gosh darn cute. I could eat you."

After I allowed Maggie to tug at my heart, I reluctantly pulled myself away and headed for the front door. "Ricky!" I shouted. I grabbed my keys from the table by the door. But I caught my reflection in the full-length mirror standing back to check myself one more time—smiling. After fluffing my hair with my fingers, I smoothed out the light pink pastel summer dress I had chosen to wear and neared the mirror to check my lipstick and mascara. It was the only makeup I wore. I was going fresh again. I smiled one more time at myself in the mirror and put on my black leather jacket draped over the couch.

Satisfied with my wardrobe, I turned my head when I heard
Ricky's footsteps coming down the stairs. My first thought was,
damn, I'm a lucky woman. I'm going to marry that beautiful man.
So I watched with a full heart and admired the crisp white shirt he
had chosen to wear with his form-fitting black jeans and black
boots. "Damn, you are gorgeous," I said, licking my lips.

"I'm thinking the same about you," he said, giving me a light
kiss on the cheek. "I don't want to ruin that lipstick of yours. I'll
save that for later." He patted my behind and gave it a pinch. "Are
you ready to go?" He said as he grabbed his keys off the small table.

I quickly grabbed his hand and took his keys. "Oh no, you
don't." I laughed as I held up the keys to my pink Mustang. "We are
taking my car tonight." Again, I laughed as I jingled them in front
of him.

Ricky shook his head and laughed. "Don't do this to me. You're
kidding, right?"

"Nope, I'm not kidding. So tonight, you get to ride in my car."

Ricky rolled his eyes. "Seriously. You are going to do this to me.
Everyone is going to be there, and you want me to pull up in a
pink car. Man, you are an evil woman." He joked. "Tell you what,
I'll meet you halfway. I'll ride in your car but don't you dare ask me
to drive it."

"Deal!" I grabbed his hand. "Come on, let's go."

"I can't believe you are making me do this. Ricky chuckled as
he crouched down in the passenger seat. I need a hat."

I gave him a friendly slap. "Oh, stop it. My car is beautiful." I
said as I pulled out of the driveway.

It took us just over twenty minutes to drive to the restaurant,
and I laughed out loud when I saw who was getting out of a car
two spaces from us. "Look, there are Claire and Travis."

Ricky quickly turned his head and covered his face. "Oh, you
have got to be kidding me."

"Hey, Claire!" I shouted from my car as I stepped out.

"Sssh, Travis will see me," Ricky said.

Travis reacted first to my voice and strolled over to my car, and laughed when he saw Ricky cowered in his seat. "How the hell did you get him to ride in your car?"

Ricky gave him a sarcastic laugh. "Hey, man. I'm not here. It's a figment of your imagination." Ricky joked. "Let me get out of this pink tutu."

Travis stood back and patted Ricky as he stepped out of the Mustang. "You got balls, bro." Travis laughed.

Ricky gave him a friendly hug. "I think I lost them in that car. Hey, you are looking good, man. You had us worried there for a while." Ricky said to Travis as he took my hand.

"Yeah. I'm feeling pretty good. A little slow on my feet, but every day, I'm feeling a little better. But, again, I want to thank both of you for watching out for Claire and being there for her."

"No need to thank us, Travis," Ricky replied. "Come on, let's get away from this car and go inside."

Slater booked a private room with an ocean view. It was away from the loud noise of the restaurant. He, Sabela, and Scottie were already there with who I recognized as Sabela's mother, Charlotte. Sabela stood first and came to greet us as we took a seat. I sat across from Charlotte and smiled at her. "Hey, Charlotte, I've not seen you in a long time. I didn't know you were coming."

She matched my smile. "When Sabela told me about the accident, I was so worried. I've met Travis a few times, and I know how much Sabela and Slater think of him. So when Sabela invited me, I wanted to be here and celebrate with you all."

"I'm glad you did." I glanced over at Scottie. "Hey, Scottie. How are you doing, buddy?"

"Good."

When Travis walked into the room holding hands with Claire, Slater left the table to greet him and hugged him. "You look great, Travis. Come on; we have a seat for you at the top of the table."

"My mom and dad should be here soon." Claire announced as she took a seat next to Travis.

"Oh, I'm so happy they will be here." I chirped. "They were so upset when I saw them at the hospital. I've been meaning to ask how they are doing."

"They are doing much better. Mom just loves Travis. He's the one that brought us back together. I have a lot to thank him for."

I didn't want to steal the show and announce our engagement too early. We were all there to celebrate Travis's recovery and give him the attention he needed after his horrendous accident, and we did. We laughed and joked, drank wine, and had cocktails. But, of course, Travis stuck to drinking orange juice. It felt good to be surrounded by good friends. Friends that I could honestly say were family.

When dessert was served, Ricky whispered in my ear. "Do you want me to tell them?"

Sabela saw him whisper. "What are you two whispering about over there?"

I blushed and giggled.

"Come on, tell us." Slater echoed.

Ricky took my hand and gave me a loving smile that melted my heart. "We have an announcement to make," Ricky said with a huge smile.

The table went silent, and all eyes were on us—even Scottie's.

Ricky looked at me again as he spoke. "Jill and I are engaged to be married."

"What! Oh my god." Sabela squealed. "Oh, I'm so happy for the two of you."

"When did this happen?" Claire said. "I just saw you last night? This is wonderful news."

I wiped the tears from my cheeks. "When I came home from work tonight, he greeted me with the most beautiful Golden Retriever puppy we named Maggie, and she had this." I held up my hand. "A gorgeous ring attached to her collar."

"Wow! Ricky, I didn't know you were such a romantic." Claire piped as she took my hand and admired the ring.

"I was so upset when Tilly left he surprised me not only with a puppy but a proposal too."

Tears poured from my eyes when Slater stood and raised his glass. "To Ricky and Jill."

We all raised our glasses. "Thank you, everyone." I cried. "We love you all so much."

"Have you set a date?" Sabela asked.

I shook my head. "No, it all happened so fast, right before we came here." I turned and looked at Ricky. "We'll set a date soon."

Sabela turned and smiled at Slater. "I have an idea, and you don't have to say anything tonight. You can think about it for a while if you want." She released a slight chuckle. "I haven't even talked to Slater about it. It just popped into my head. He may not like my idea, but I'm going to throw it out there."

Again the table went silent, and we listened to Sabela pitch her idea to us.

"This is not just to Ricky and Jill but to Travis and Claire too."

Travis and Claire looked at each other with creased brows, wondering what Sabela was about to say.

"Slater and I have been engaged for almost two years now. Travis and Claire recently got engaged, and now Ricky and Jill are engaged. So we have three weddings to look forward to." She hesitated. "Or just one."

"Just one?" I asked, sounding confused.

"Look, guys, we have gone through so much together in the past few years. My horrific ordeal with Davin. The death of Eve and discovering Slater is Scottie's father. Claire lost a brother but found Travis, who helped her reunite with her parents. Both of you want a family and may run a foster home for us someday. And then recently, we all bonded together when Travis had his accident. Even Jill and Claire are now the best of friends, which I never thought I'd live to see ever happening."

Slater butted in. "Sabela, what are you trying to say?"

"Look, we have shared so much together. I think it would be really special if we share our wedding day."

"What?" Slater asked. "You mean we all get married on the same day?"

"Not just on the same day, but at the same ceremony. A triple wedding."

Slater leaned back in his chair with his mouth open.

No one answered. We were all deep in thought.

Travis spoke first. "A triple wedding. I like that idea."

Sabela's eyes lit up. "You do."

Claire smiled and took Travis's hand. "I do too. I think it's brilliant. Where would you think of having it?"

"At sunset on the beach," Sabela said as she looked over at Slater, who still had not said a word. "It was our original plan."

"I love that. How romantic." Claire said, turning to me. "What do you think, guys? Are you in?"

I looked at Ricky. "What do you think?"

Ricky nodded and smiled at everyone. "I think it's a fantastic idea. I can't think of any better people I'd love to share my wedding with."

"Oh, Ricky, I was hoping you would say yes." I cried.

Sabela looked at Slater, who had yet to give a yay or nay. "Well, Slater. What do you say? Do you like the idea of a triple wedding on the beach with some of our closest friends?"

He leaned in and cupped her face in his hands before kissing her passionately on the lips. "I think it's a beautiful idea. Let's get married."

Cheers let loose at the table, and glasses were raised. Well, guys, it looks like we have a triple wedding to plan.

ABOUT THE AUTHOR

**ABOUT THE AUTHOR**

Tina Hogan Grant loves to write stories with strong female characters that know what they want and aren't afraid to chase their dreams. She loves to write sexy and sometimes steamy romances with happy ever after endings.

She is living life to the fullest in a small mountain community in Southern California with her husband and two dogs. When she is not writing she is probably riding her ATV, kayaking or hiking with her best friend – her husband of twenty-five years.

www.tinahogangrant.com